MY ADVENTUROUS TIMES IN ANTARCTICA

MY PERSONAL EXPERIENCE WITH THE 'AUSTRALIAN NATIONAL ANTARCTIC RESEARCH EXPEDITION (ANARE)'

Macquarie Island 1978 (Wintered & '79 Summer)
&
Casey 1981 Station (Wintered)

Lance M Olsen

Publisher: Inspiring Publishers,
P.O. Box 159, Calwell, ACT Australia 2905
Email: publishaspg@gmail.com
http://www.inspiringpublishers.com

A catalogue record for this
book is available from the
National Library of Australia

National Library of Australia The Prepublication Data Service

Author: Lance M Olsen
Title: My Adventurous Times in Antarctica
Genre: Non-fiction, Memoir
ISBN: 978-1-922792-21-1

Author: Lance Olsen

CONTENTS

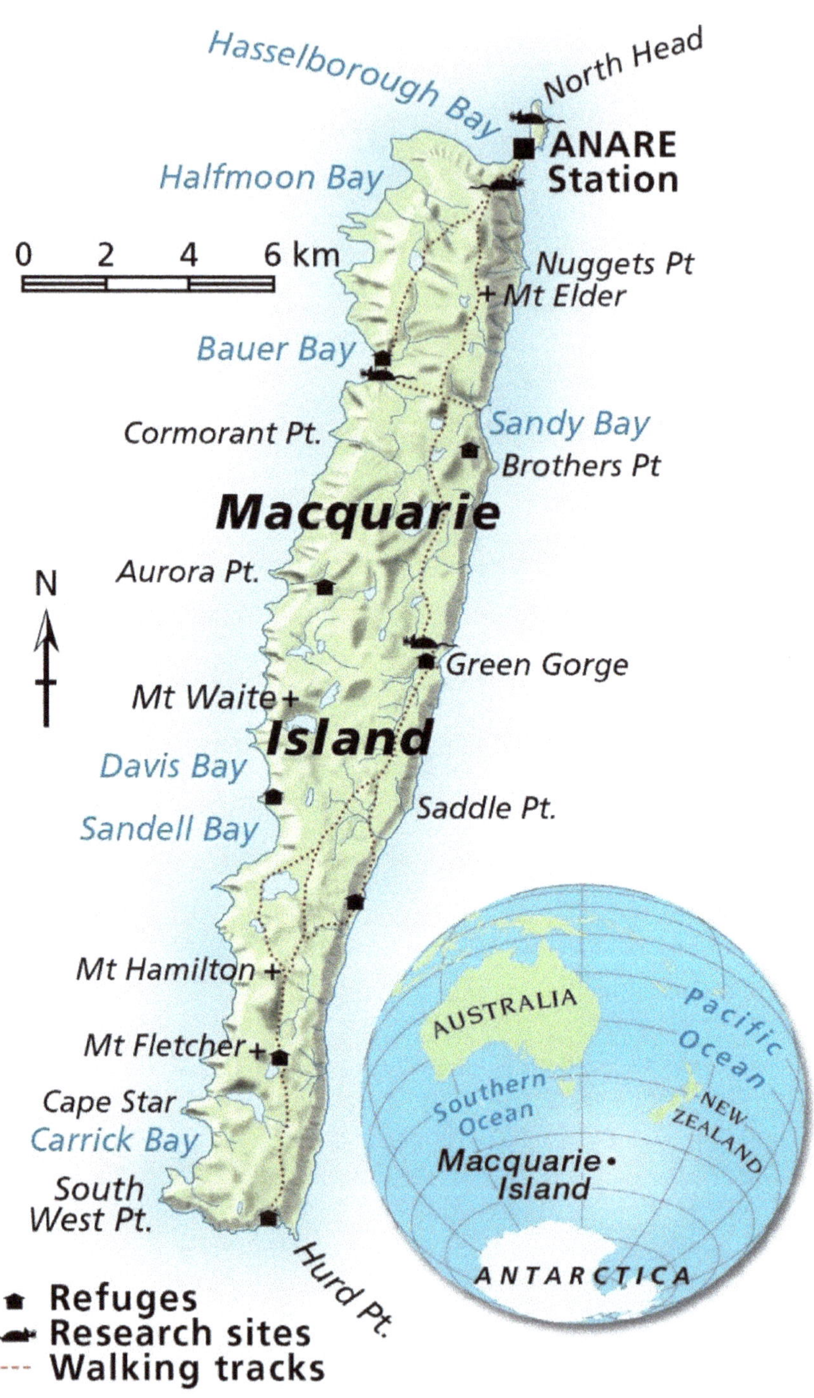

Picture courtesy of Blogspot.com (Post 1979).

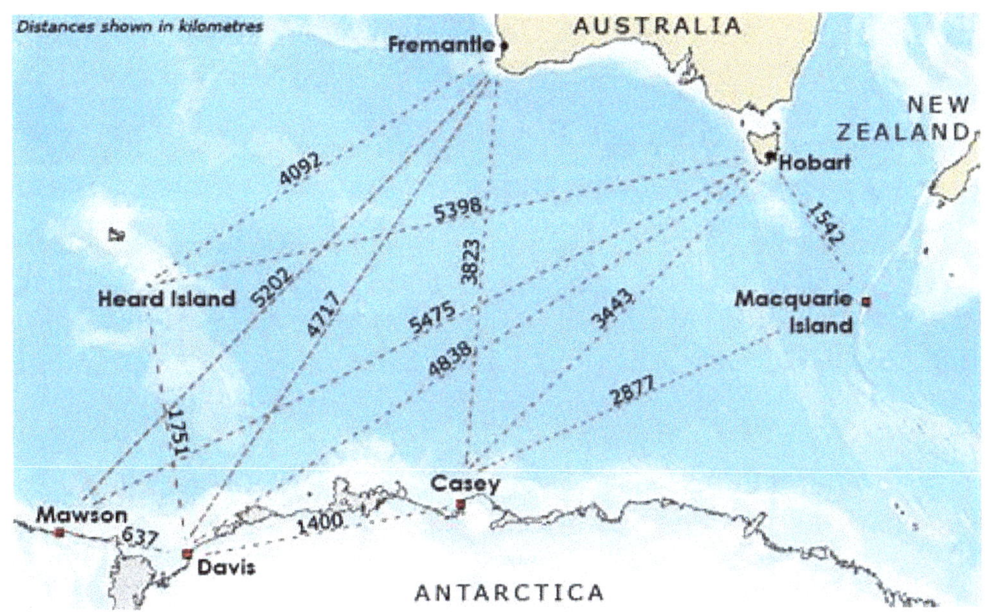

Courtesy of johnkellyartist.com.
(The Australian Antarctic and sub-Antarctic stations)

INTRODUCTION

I boarded the ice breaker ship, the *Thala Dan* in the summer of 1979, after she serviced the other Australian Science Research Stations in Antarctica. Seeing Australia for the first time in 15 months after being stationed at the Sub-Antarctic Macquarie Island, was going to be an unknown, as I had changed and where would my life take me now? I returned to The Overseas Telecommunications Commission international exchange in Paddington, Sydney and a year later, my desire to return to the Australian Antarctic Division brought about my new adventure to the Antarctic continent. Casey Station 1981.

Much of my life has been an adventure, with the ups and downs associated with it. I do like challenges and the writing of this book is one. I am now retired and enjoying life without the pressures of and routines and distractions of technical work. Now that I am out of electronics and communications engineering field, I am developing another side of myself. Having completed a Medical Intuitive Healing certificate and diploma course, I now realise that there is more to life than the logic, materialism, and the information world that we live in. Being alive, learning, living, and sharing on this planet of ours, is a gift. We need to nurture ourselves and this planet and strive to be happy with both. I am now looking forward to new challenges.

CHAPTER 1

THE AUSTRALIAN ANTARCTIC DIVISION (MACQUARIE ISLAND STATION 1978/'79 - 15 MONTHS)

Darwin Coastal Radio Station. (Overseas Telecommunications Commission – Australia.).

Who would ever believe that life would change so dramatically by happening upon a newspaper advertisement?

I had just completed a stint in Darwin, post Cyclone Tracy (Christmas of 1974) which had destroyed the city where I was maintaining on my own the Darwin Coastal Radio Station (OTC Aust.). Prior to this, I had almost completed my cadetship with The Overseas Telecommunications Commission in Brisbane when I was transferred to Sydney in 1975 to complete my final year. I heard that the Radio Technical Officer Gd. 2 in charge of maintaining the Darwin Coastal Radio Station, wanted to leave the station after having lost his house previously in the cyclone. I approached the Chief Engineer in head office in Martin Place, Sydney for a possible transfer to Darwin, to maintain this station single-handed, even though I wasn't quite out of my training. The Chief Engineer agreed after the interview. I stayed in this position at Darwin CRS for 18 months, gaining valuable experience in the radio field. Later this was to be important for my future career path. Many of my fellow students later went on to the IT field earning better wages. I preferred to remain in the electronics and communications field which is what I found exciting and an essential service.

Courtesy of blogspot.com (Effects of Cyclone Tracy, Christmas 1974)

Always with a sense of spirit of adventure, I left Darwin on my motor bike to return to Sydney, 3,200km. On the way, I arrived in Cairns for the night after riding through mostly rain as this was the wet season for the northern part of Australia. The next morning while drying off my clothes and camping equipment, I bought a local Cairns newspaper. I read that the Australian Antarctic Division (Department of science), was asking for Radio Operators to join the expeditions to Antarctica and Macquarie Island. There were four Science Research Stations under the control of the Division (Macquarie Island, Casey, Mawson, and Davis Stations), and the expeditioners were then to be part of the Australian National Antarctic Expedition (ANARE). With great excitement and a sense of adventure sharpened by my extended motor bike ride, I sealed the envelope that would soon determine my future one way or another. I sent off the letter to the Antarctic Division (Melbourne), asking to be considered for a position as a Radio Operator, of which I knew they'd decline, as I was technical. So, it was just a joke into the exciting dream of an adventurer. The problem was my application was taken seriously. It was no longer a joke. I was going from literally one extreme to another, at least climate-wise, from tropical Darwin to sub-zero freezing temperatures.

I arrived in Sydney, after a brief stay with my family in Brisbane, where I received a phone call from the Antarctic Division, to fly down to Melbourne Antarctic Division asap, as there was a position for an experienced Radio Technical Officer to be the RADIO OIC of Macquarie Island, complete with two Radio Operators and the Radio Station itself. Macquarie is a Sub Antarctic Science Research Station below Hobart and halfway down to the Antarctic Continent. And in the Convergence zone of the South Pacific Ocean and the Southern Ocean. The environment was to be cold and very wet, due to the 315 days of about 980mm of precipitation that it is subjected to, and almost constant, unending high winds, the 'furious 50s' as it was referred to. I had no idea as to what I was getting myself into and decided to be adventurous and go along with the flow. I was a little disappointed with not going down to the Antarctic Continent, but as I knew nothing about either, I was off to Macquarie Island anyway. I did manage to do some basic survival training in the Snowy mountains, mandatory medical checks, and tests by a psychiatrist to see why I wanted to go and that I would get on well with other expeditioners. Curiosity is one of my strongest traits, and this was an opportunity to find out what it was like to winter with just 19 other expeditioners and discover new territory outside of Australia and discover new personal dimensions. There was little time at the Division in Melbourne for training, before embarking on the *Nella Dan*, a Danish ice breaker ship. As I had the technical knowledge required from my experience in Darwin Coastal Radio Station, I was very suited for Macquarie communications centre, being similar in a technical sense. The Darwin Coastal Radio Station was close to the Darwin City coastline, which experienced salt air corrosion from the ocean salt breezes to the radio antennas, masts, and radio equipment inside the station. So was Macquarie Island radio station! It was going to be very much a challenge in maintaining this station, which was to be the equivalent to the adventure that I was on.

Macquarie Island 1978 (15 months)

Above: Macquarie Island 1978.

I left the Melbourne docks on the *Nella Dan*, a Danish Ice breaker, after being farewelled by my girlfriend and parents.

It was ok sailing out into the Bass Strait, though it soon became very rough, and the ship was rolling from side to side greatly.

Above two pictures show us leaving Melbourne aboard the *Nella Dan.*

I was on the top deck enjoying the rough seas, when I decided to go into the observation room on the very top of the ship, above the Wheelhouse or Bridge. As people regularly smoked in those days, many on board the ship would go into the observation room for a quiet smoke and chat. I entered the room and soon became ill and green from inhaling the secondary smoke in the air. A quick exit to fresh air was needed. After sailing through the rough seas to Macquarie, I noticed that there were very few expeditioners in the dining room during mealtimes. I was wondering whether we were a mentally and physically tough mob, or just beginners on an epic voyage to the unknown.

The *Nella Dan* sailed on for several days rolling up to 45 degrees, making it difficult or impossible to sleep unless you became a dead weight from exhaustion and sleep thereafter. The ships propeller would often be spinning in the air at the peak of the waves, and one would be looking up at the top of the waves when we went into the trough of the wave. This pattern continued until we reached the island. We were greeted by fog encapsulating the island, with only the sandy isthmus showing signs that there must be life, somewhere in the buildings that were only just visible.

CHAPTER 2

ARRIVAL AT MACQUARIE ISLAND

This picture shows the station is built on an isthmus. Macquarie Island Research Station – "The Jewel of the South Pacific". (On a sunny day, that is).

Reaching the shore line on the ADF Army LARCs (Lighter Amphibious Resupply Cargo), amphibian vehicles, used for supplying the island with essentials and expeditioners, was a hazardous affair, especially going through the rough coastal surf. I had great respect for the army LARC soldiers for their skills in keeping us afloat and not tipping over in the rough surf.

After being greeted by the 1977 expeditioners, getting a run down on the operation of the station, and talking to the outgoing Radio OIC (radio technician) and the three radio operators (one being a female), we attended the change-over ceremony. We then saw them off to the *Nella Dan* which was to return them back to Australia. As I watched the *Nella Dan* turn and head out to the deep wild ocean from where we came, I realised and felt that this was going to be home, and no going back for a year or more. My feelings were quite palpable as I was filled with excitement and a modicum of uncertainty.

The above image shows the Army Larc transporting us to the island station.

The above image shows *Nella Dan* during the transporting the expeditioners to and from the island, and the suppliers being brought over on the Army LARCs.

The above image are the expeditioners climbing down the side of the ship to the waiting Army LARCs.

As seen, we were an international group to a degree as depicted by the flags. We are shown here (below pictures), unloading the ship with our 18 months' worth of supplies (an extra 6 months' supply of food and hardware, were in case the ship couldn't get back the following year to pick us up!) by the Army LARCs, and a barge for the heavy machinery necessary to put up a new science building, and other tasks.

The twenty 1978 winter expeditioners consisted of: Station OIC, Doctor, Cook, Building Supervisor, Carpenter, Diesel Mechanic, Plumber, Brick Layer, Meteorology OIC, Meteorology Observers, Meteorology Technician, Radio OIC, Radio Operators, Biologist, Geologist, Auroral Physicist, marine divers (scientists).

The list of 1978/79 expeditioners names are found on page 99/100.

Above is the diesel fuel flexible pipeline going from the *Nella Dan* to the station diesel storage tanks on shore.

A pipeline went from the *Nella Dan* to the shore, pumping diesel fuel to the fuel tanks, that was also to last us for the duration of our stay on the island. The fuel was for the two large diesel generators that provided us with electrical power, and the diesel generators also provided hot water to heat some of the buildings. There were also two smaller operational generators for emergency use, left over from previous years.

Above is a view of the diesel fuel tanks in the distance, necessary for storing and supplying diesel fuel to the generators. The Meteorology radar dome and the new arrived expeditioners are delivered by the Army LARC.

Above is an Army LARC doing the supply run to the station and to the coastal field huts in treacherous surf, as well as the expeditioners transportation to and from the *Nella Dan.*

Unloading necessities.

Most of the food unloaded consisted of frozen meats and vegetables, cans containing food of sorts, alcohol for special occasions, beer ingredients supplied by a Carlton and United Breweries', and fresh fruit and vegetables that would last only a short time in the cold room. Some plants and food were grown in the green house such as tomatoes and lettuce, etc.). Though I could never understand how the green house worked, as there was less than 40 days of non-precipitous weather and some sunshine a year. It was located next to the sleeping quarters (dongas).

Above shows the Green House and the sleeping quarters (dongas).

These scenes located in the dongas are, bathroom and laundry in 1978.

The clear weather period was the time to take photos depicting Macquarie Island in her apparent splendour. "The Jewel of the South Pacific" as she was fondly called by the expeditioners. Or just 'Macca'. No one at home would ever think that this island had mostly howling winds, wet and drizzly, and foggy conditions most of the time. Extra clothing was brought ashore as there would be demands to replace worn clothing and Antarctic weather gear during the year. A trip around the island (which was about 34 km by 5 km) by these Army LARCs would supply the 6 field huts (8 field huts to date), that were used by the expeditioners on recreation, and by biologists, who studied the birds, seals, penguins, and the study of the rats, cats, and rabbits left behind by the sealers in the 19th century.

The research information from the study of these introduced animals, was used later to eradicate them. The island naturally had no predators, until the sealers brought them to the island for food and pets. And the sealers themselves eradicated the fur seal population and severely reduced the penguin and elephant seal populations just for their oil. These introduced animals, rats, cats, and rabbits were a problem, eating the birds and their eggs, eating the unique island vegetation, and digging into the soft soil around the island causing soil erosion. The final eradication of these dangerous animals was declared in 2011. (No sightings of these animals since).

Above is the Biologist whose job was to study the wildlife on the island, pictured working in one of the field huts.

The island was about 34km long and 5 km wide. There was a 300 metres climb every morning to get up onto the plateau, necessary to traverse the island for whatever reason you had. I needed to check all the field huts radio transceivers, batteries, and antennas every 3 months. It was a 10-day trip each time for me, which I enjoyed very much, especially the rough weather and wildlife. The survival confidence, and the fitness it brought me was immeasurable. I was only 24 years old.

Above picture of myself attending to one of the field hut's radio antennas.

Above is our water supply from the plateau to the Station. 1978. Des, our doctor, inspecting the small dam.

The Division's budget was tight in those days, as much of the budget was for the supply ships, supplies, clothing, and wages. So much was done with little on the stations and maximised by the highly talented expeditioners selected in their field. i.e., the support crew and scientists. Those support staff in the Division back in Melbourne (now located in Kingston, Tasmania), were usually expeditioners themselves, and knew the conditions and equipment that were needed for us to do our job in these harsh environments. So, we were still in pioneering days with our limited technology compared with today's station facilities, and support and scientific equipment. Though the environment hasn't changed much since then. So, venturing outside still encompasses the dangers one would expect.

When I first landed on Macquarie Island, wages were 30% higher than those at the maximum rate back in Australia. Soon after arrival, the Division raised the wages to 80% of the maximum rate back in Australia. This was enough for me to put a deposit on a terrace house in Alexandria, Sydney. As there was nothing to spend my earnings on except for radio calls, and telexes when the radio conditions were right. There was no internet and satellite communication like today.

The three Australian Antarctic Research Stations are necessary for Australia to lay claim on much of the continent, and to contribute much valuable science of our planet and outer space and weather research. The stations are all manned constantly with a changeover of expeditioners each year. More on Antarctic life will be explained later in my experiences on Casey Station, 1981 later in this book.

Macquarie Island is a wildlife reserve and has a scientific research and weather station. Macquarie Island, a UNESCO World Heritage Site, lies in the Southwestern Pacific Ocean, about halfway between Australia and Antarctica. Regionally part of Oceania and politically a part of Tasmania, Australia, since 1900, it became a Tasmanian State Reserve in 1978 and was inscribed on the World Heritage List in 1997. Macquarie Island, a volcanic mass with an area of 123 square km (47 square miles) and a general elevation of 240 meters (800 feet), measures 34 km x 5 km (21 x 3 miles) and has several rocky islets offshore. It is subjected to the occasional earthquake and in 2004, an earthquake measured 8.1. The island is located right on the Australian plate and Pacific plate.

Weather at Macquarie Island was generally 3 to 7 degrees Celsius constant mean temperature for majority of the year. At times it went below zero. Precipitation 315 days, 980mm. The average monthly average wind speed was 48 to 56 km/hr. Winds would at times be such that one could not walk up straight. Once I was caught at the Radio Hut in howling winds and needed to return to the mess that night. Much of the walk back consisted of crawling on my hands and knees. Luckily the two streetlights showed me the way back to the mess. And the ocean swell would flow over the isthmus between the science buildings, workshops, radio hut, and the living areas of the station.

Courtesy of https://escales.ponant.com/en/roaring-40s-furious-50s/

Above picture describes the location of the roaring 40s (Tasmania), furious 50s (Macquarie Island) and screaming 60s (Antarctica).

Macquarie Island coastline consists of large surf swells. The ocean water at the beaches is about 5 degrees Celsius. We needed to jump in and wash and bath ourselves whilst down at the island huts. Not for the faint hearted. There is no way to traverse around the coastline. So, one had to be very fit to climb up the 300 metres slopes to the plateau, then down when we had reached our destination field hut location for the night.

Above is the Station in the background located on the isthmus, and the typical coastline one would have to climb up when traversing the island each day, below.

According to one biologist, Macquarie Island Cabbage which is prolific around the coastline is possible to eat. Also, the sea Kelp located along the coastal line, is edible, but the acid content would eat away your teeth enamel. Tussock grass was also prolific on the island.

Above is the seaweed 'Kelp', along the coastal shoreline.

Above is the Macquarie Island Cabbage. Engulfed in the cabbage is one of our volunteer ornithologists. Summer of 1979.

The terrain: 'RUGGED', 'BARREN', ISOLATED', HARSH WEATHER.

Above shows that the winds were strong on this ridge. Commonly called then, 'Windy Ridge'.

Above is the view of the station from the plateau. Author with the female cook, Enid.

Above shows the typical 300 metres climb from the field hut to the plateau.

The two images above show the typical terrain on the island plateau.

The picture above shows the coastal ruggedness. Impossible to walk around the island via the coast. Hence the need to climb up to the plateau and down again to wherever we were going.

The picture above shows the author in contemplation, at Nuggets Point. The station is in the background. Tussock grass behind me.

Above are some of these lakes that can freeze over during the winter months. An early expeditioner lost his life when he skied out onto the ice and went through it to the bottom. His grave is still by the lake.

Above we assumed was a sealer's grave from the 19ᵗʰ or 20ᵗʰ century. No markings except for stones. One of our carpenters built a fence around the grave.

Above is the 'feather bed' is comprised of dense moss on the ground, some located on the coastal plains and much on the plateau. It is centuries old of rotting vegetation/moss/mud several metres deep. One of our expeditioners made the mistake of walking off the firm moss bed, onto the soft moss bed and went up to his waist in bog. It really stinks and it's a long way to walk back to the station in this condition.

Some Macquarie Island history:

From the first recorded landfall by man in 1810, Macquarie Island was regarded as a valuable source of riches. Sealers first targeted seals and Macquarie's original fur seal population was hunted to extinction in just ten years.

Almost 100 ships and their gangs worked at Macquarie Island for 20 years, hunting relentlessly. Elephant seals were also rendered down in pots to recover their oil for use as a lighting fuel, machine lubricant and a component in tanning and rope making processes.

The focus of exploitation eventually moved from elephant seals to penguins and by 1905 there were steam digester plants yielding about 500ml of oil. The arrival of the Australasian Antarctic Expedition in 1911 triggered pressure to end the animal oil industry and the licence was revoked in 1919.

Scientific interest in the island had begun nearly 100 years before with collections of flora and fauna specimens and mapping of the coastline. Several other visits followed but it was geologist Douglas Mawson's fascination with the island that led to there being a small research base on the isthmus between 1911 and 1914. A wireless link to Hobart was established and the base was used to study Macquarie Island's natural attributes as well as recording meteorological data.

In 1948 the Australian government built a scientific station on the island, and this has been in operation ever since. Macquarie Island's strategic position surrounded by a cold ocean and clean air makes data collected on the island uniquely valuable in weather forecasting and atmospheric monitoring. It is an important site for studies of the ionosphere and upper atmospheric monitoring, including observations of the ozone layer. Also, radio frequencies measured from outer space.

The amazing changes on Macquarie Island at present times are best illustrated by the futuristic grey bubble of the ANARSAT dome. It collects satellite communications signals not far from the rusting digesters that once turned seals and penguins into oil.

It was Douglas Mawson who instigated the stop to the animal oil industry on Macquarie Island, and he influenced the transfer of the island to that of a Tasmanian National Park status.

Pictures above shows the digesters used for boiling down seals and penguins by the sealers for their oil. Located at the 'The Nuggets', Macquarie Island, 1978.

These relics are a reminder of the time when there was little regard for wildlife apart from commercial gain.

The sealing era on the island lasted from 1810 to 1919, during which time 144 vessel visits are recorded, twelve of which ended in shipwreck. There is a cave on the island that I explored, where I found bones of birds left there which appeared to be very old and weathered. Possibly left by the stranded sealers when they hunted for wildlife to feed themselves, and before their eventual rescue.

CHAPTER 3

DAILY ROUTINES

Radio operations were not smooth sailing initially when we took over the radio communications on the Island. I was trained in Melbourne to type on a telex machine, to assist in covering the required 24-hour scheduled shifts on Macquarie Island, as there were only two radio operators and myself this year. The radio circuit later became 24 hours continuous leased radio circuit instead of only having scheduled linkups during the day and night by the radio operators. Which meant the Meteorological (Met) staff could get their own telex messages and weather reports out when required during the night shifts. And there were no requirements for the radio operators to handle the weather traffic at night, once the 24-hour lease came into effect. I couldn't type fast enough as much of the weather traffic was in numeral code. Thus, the radio operators decided to do the 2 x 12 hour shifts themselves with one operator short. This was soon resolved, and the radio operators stopped their 12-hour night shifts once the continuous 24 hour leased circuit came into effect, I mainly left the radio operators to otherwise do their job, as they were proficient and handled the communications traffic, voice, and telex well.

As Radio OIC, I felt that there was little need to intervene with the running of the radio operations due to any incompetencies from the two operators. Many times, I had to close communications due to equipment failure, antennae blown down in blizzards, or just the old standby valve transmitter arced over when an operator tuned it up wrongly. This tuning was an art form and sometimes had to be done by me. I had many a laugh when the room lit up in multiple colours from this old transmitter, when the tuning went wrong, or the antenna broke in wild weather. I knew that the arcing across a large, soldered joint on the main tuning coil would slowly evaporate, giving off a spectacular glow of colours. No damage to the transmitter other than the vaporised solder which was easily replaced.

There was a large electrical heater box inside the front door of the radio hut, just large enough for me to lie on after a long spell working outside, as the exposure from the weather was severe, chilling one down to the bones.

Sometimes when any of the men came in for a 'radio schedule' or sending out a personal telex (which they had to pay for on return to the mainland as OTC (Aust.) which they were charged by the number of characters sent, or the time spent on radio voice calls), they'd see me lying on top of this heater box, thawing out. We had several 5 letter codes to send as a telex message, to describe our situation or feelings which the Antarctic Division were kind enough to give us these codes, to our family and friends. These codes would save us a lot of money in charges on return to Australia. These and the radio calls were the only expenditure we had while on the station. The radio schedules were limited to time allocated. The radio operators would have a good rapport with the telephone operators in Sydney at the other end of our radio link.

Valuable scientific data was constantly being sent out via telex as well. Enabling the science researchers back in Australia to analyse this information in almost real time, daily that is.

The radio operators would have a weekly radio schedule with Campbell Island, further east below New Zealand. They were the NZ equivalent to Macquarie Island, with scientific research and a weather station. A chat and a chess game would while away the spare time the radio operators would have.

There was an emergency transceiver in one of the science huts, should there be total failure of our radio network to OTC Sydney. This transceiver (1 KW) could be tuned to any HF frequency including amateur stations in an emergency. An account of this necessary happening will be described in my time at Casey Station, Antarctica, later in my book.

Yes, that's the author above, about to get his test equipment loaded onto the tractor, and to take up to the Transmitter hut, which was at the end of the isthmus. Some repairs were necessary for the main transmitter. It was a bumpy ride for the electronic test equipment though.

"OUT" WYSSA

Pictures above and below are of the Radio Hut. The radio operator above is talking to the RAAF aircraft, coming in to do a mail drop on the island. The station OIC, diesel mechanic, brick layer in the background and myself were looking on, waiting on for further instructions from the approaching aircraft.

Here I am in the Radio hut sorting out the problems associated with the telex multiplexing rack (Teletype-on-Radio machine) in the radio shack. The tall silver rack. Directly behind me is the old standby valve type transmitter (1 KW which glows in many colours when it is not tuned correctly, or the antenna is down due to high winds conditions. The main transmitter at the end of the isthmus was fully solid state (1 KW), though physically large by today's standards.

The above old transmitter required a brave man to tune it to a new frequency.

I approached the Radio Hut one morning to do some work inside, and lo and behold, was a large elephant seal at the front of the door. A dilemma occurred within me as to how to move the seal away from the doorway, as these seals are known to settle into their spot for some time. I remembered that when two seals fight each other, the one that reaches high above the other, wins and the other seal backs off. Great I thought. I found a broom from the Met Building and brought it over to the seal. Putting the broom head above the seal made him rear up and move backwards, away from the high broom head. So, I managed to steer him away from the Radio Hut and I was able to enter the building.

Above, the remains of a mast or gantry at the top of North Head.

Sir Douglas Mawson used the island as a radio relay station, for his base in Antarctica, Commonwealth Bay in 1911.

The installation of the new 30-metre (90 foot) radio mast at the beginning of the 1979-year, was required. The mast sections were dropped off onto the beach from the supply ship for me, so as I could replace the old rusted out 30-metre mast next to the Radio Hut that I had asked for during my year. I climbed the old mast regularly to replace antennas after blizzards and wild weather. It could have broken in half while I was up it when doing repairs as it was so rusted. I found this out when I went to paint the mast, and my paint scrapper went through the side of the mast section, halfway up. Once I received the new mast sections, it was up to me to get it up with some help from the carpenter and the incoming 1979 Radio Technician (Radio OIC). The first thing to do was to dig by hand the three anchor points for the guy wires, that would soon be attached to the top mast section, and then filled with concrete. As I found out, the 1979 carpenter wasn't silly by offering to dig the first hole while I watched. I thought he was being kind and I let him go ahead. I soon found after a while, that I was freezing outside of the hole, as the cold damp conditions and wind were causing exposure problems for me, while standing, watching. I politely asked him if I could finish off the anchor hole and I got back into the hole, continued digging, trying to keep warm as well this way. Once the mast anchor holes and base were poured with concrete, a problem came as to how can we get the mast sections into position. I knew from training to lift each section of the mast up and put another one under it continuously until it was raised to 30 metres. The carpenter thought of using the forklift from the supply building which was strong enough to lift the mast sections up. The crane could steady the mast as it goes up, thereby creating a safe workplace. I thought it was a great idea and we went ahead with the raising of the mast. I have great admiration of the tradesmen sent to these research stations as support crew, as their innovations and skills are amazingly good. The scientists also obviously had amazing skills and knowledge in their own fields.

Pictured above is the dropping of the old rusted, dangerous mast, located next to the Radio Hut. The next larger building behind the radio hut was the Met observers balloon launching bay which they would send up hydrogen balloon daily with electronics on board, to measure such things a humidity, height, temperature, and air pressure. These were transmitted back to the Met observers monitoring room, where the weather information was sent back to Australia. The balloon was also tracked by a Met radar on the ground. Met had their own radar technician to look after the radar and metrology electronic equipment. He also stood in as an observer doing shift work with the others.

Above picture is of us putting up the mast, section by section.

Then it was up to me to put the antennae on top of the mast.

Macquarie Island Station, summer of 1979. The 30-metre mast above was finally raised by the three of us. Pictured are Rob (carpenter), me and John ('79 Radio OIC).

I was requested to lay a second communications signal cable to the radio transmitter hut, to be run in a trench, to be dug by the backhoe operator. I marked the approx. approximate 60-metre run with flour on the ground, in Summer obviously as the flour would be indiscernible in the white blanket of Winter snow, and I stated that it was not to be deviated from this white line. And guess what? The backhoe operator decided to make a short cut between the transmitter hut and the radio hut, cutting our only operational cable to the radio hut. I spent hours in the freezing, wet, and cold night in the trench, trying to join the multiple stands of fine wires in the cable together. My fingers were frozen so much so that I could hardly move them. When I got up to walk, I couldn't as my legs were almost frozen as well. So, I hobbled back to the station mess to thaw out again. I was not happy that evening! I had further trouble, when I found that the main radio transmitter hut had a fan blowing in cold salt laden air, slowly but surely corroding the new solid-state transmitter. The carpenter then installed the split air-conditioner in the transmitter hut for me.

Above picture shows the newly dug cable trench to the remote transmitter hut pictured.

Macquarie radio duties and responsibilities were the toughest I have ever come across in my career. So much of the equipment and masts and antennae were old and corrosion had set into various radio and electronic equipment as well. This kept me busy the whole year. Sometimes I would miss out on the social events happening due to this work demand and the essential service I had to perform. Three years later, I returned to Macquarie Island for a day, on the voyage back to Hobart from Casey Station in 1982. I read up in the radio log of 1979 that there was little for the radio technician to do during the year, as I had already left the radio station in excellent condition. This made me feel very happy with my efforts. The 1982 Macquarie radio technician, mentioned to me, that some radio technician had it hard in 1978, after reading the radio technical logs. I said, 'yes he did'.

The meteorology operators would make hydrogen for the balloons that would be sent into the atmosphere to measure various things such as height, barometer, humidity, temperature, etc, and the balloon would be tracked manually via a radar on the ground. If the winds on the ground were high, several attempts would be made to launch the balloons. If no success, the balloon launching would be abandoned. It was interesting watching this, especially when the winds were high. The balloon would bounce in every direction in the observer's hands. I watched in horror, as one Met Observer who was trying to launch the balloon from the balloon shed, fell, and slid in the snow. Another time, the balloon shed's front doors collapsed inwards due to the howling winds. Luckily the Met Observer was standing at the rear of the shed, out of harm's way at the time.

The biologists spent most of the year living down the island, studying the introduced animals and vermin that were destroying the terrain, vegetation, and wildlife. These animals were introduced by the sealers. Also, the study consisted of the numbers of seals, birds, and penguins. And their weights and measurements and general health. Several elephant seals during the year were killed and studied for such things as internal parasites, and other internal affectations to their health. I participated in catching penguins and weighing them, measuring their beaks, etc. These penguins were tough animals. Once they get their flipper out of your hold, you would get hammered severely with the flippers until you were bruised badly. Many an indignant penguin I have seen, after being released.

Above, I am holding one penguin, being prepared to be measured and weighed. 1978.

Some of the physicist's roles were to measure the micro pulsations from space, and film the auroras at night on an 'all sky camera', and other projects. I was instrumental in getting this 'all sky camera' working early in the year, as in the previous year, they were unable to get it working, hence losing out on valuable filming of auroras. I found that a 240V relay would arc over inside its housing within the camera chassis, creating electrical radiation interference with the electronics of the machine. I had nothing to redesign the circuit with, so I tipped the relay unit upside down and filled it with oil to suppress the arcing of the contacts. It worked. I was pleased to have done my job for this research program, and that was all I needed.

Above is the 'All Sky Camera' hut view of the station. 1978.

The female living quarters were completed a year before I arrived at Macquarie. Our year had to complete the food, vehicles, and materials supply building near the living area of the station. The carpenters then had to build the new science building in the vicinity of the Radio Hut, weather station and workshops. There were two carpenters and one brick layer to do the job, and willing hands when required.

Above is the supply and storage building completion. 1978

Above is the long science building under construction in 1978.

Above is a view from the unfinished science build of the station during a blizzard.

Above picure is the electricity contol panel to the station buildings.

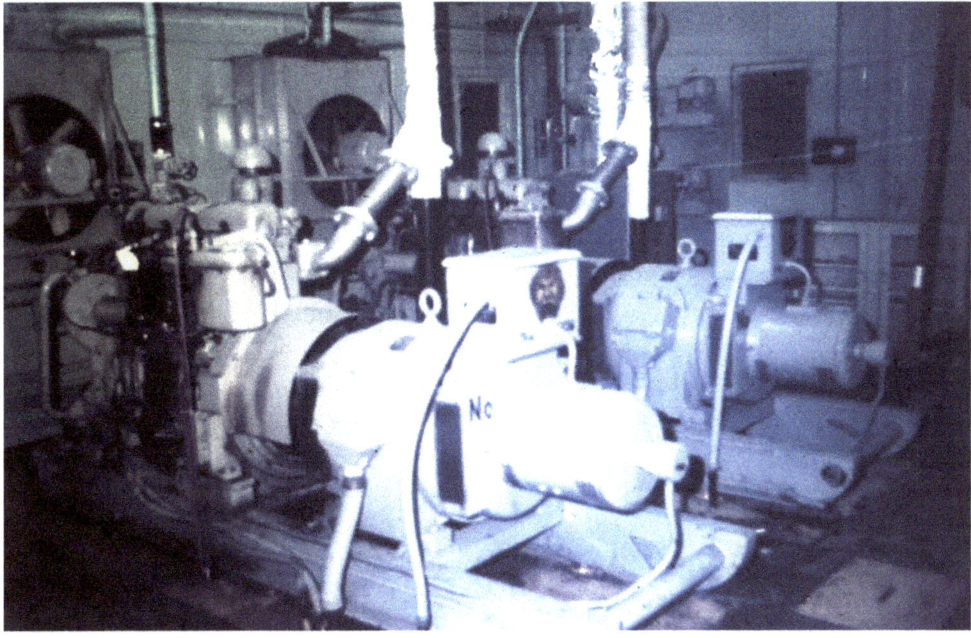

Above, are two large diesel generators which supplied 240V electricity to all the buildings and the two streetlights. The hot water from the generators was piped through to the living areas at this end of the station only. Heating to the working and science buildings used the electricity from these generators as in electric heaters, and for the operating radio, meteorology, and science equipment.

When the weather is good, and your journey takes you past vast colonies of penguins, seals, and sea birds, on your way to the six iconic Macquarie Island field huts, it's just beautiful.

Some of the huts in 1978 were just very large wooden boxes used to house machinery, etc from previous trips to the island, modified by carpenters to include bunks, kitchenette if you call it that, kerosene stove for cooking and heating and drying off wet clothes, and storage for tinned food, either carried down by backpacks, or dropped off by an Army LARC, at the beginning of the summer. These army soldiers driving the Army LARC through treacherous surf, were as brave as they come. Several other huts were larger having been previously designed and supplied by the Antarctic Division. Wind generators, or batteries carried down the island to the huts were to power radio transceivers. Huts were stocked with food for twelve months or more. Kerosene was needed for cooking and lighting/heating and drying of cloths, was delivered by Army LARC, or carried by backpack when supplies were low during the year.

Above five pictures are some of the island field huts in 1978.

Above two pictures show what it was like inside one of the field huts around the coastal shore line. Yes, that's me inside the huts thawing out and drying off, having a radio schedule with the station operators. Picture showing the bunks with a female volunteer ornathologist that I accompanied down the island, during the 1979 summer that I over stayed for.

Above is me baking bread in a fry pan over a keroscene stove. And making coffee.

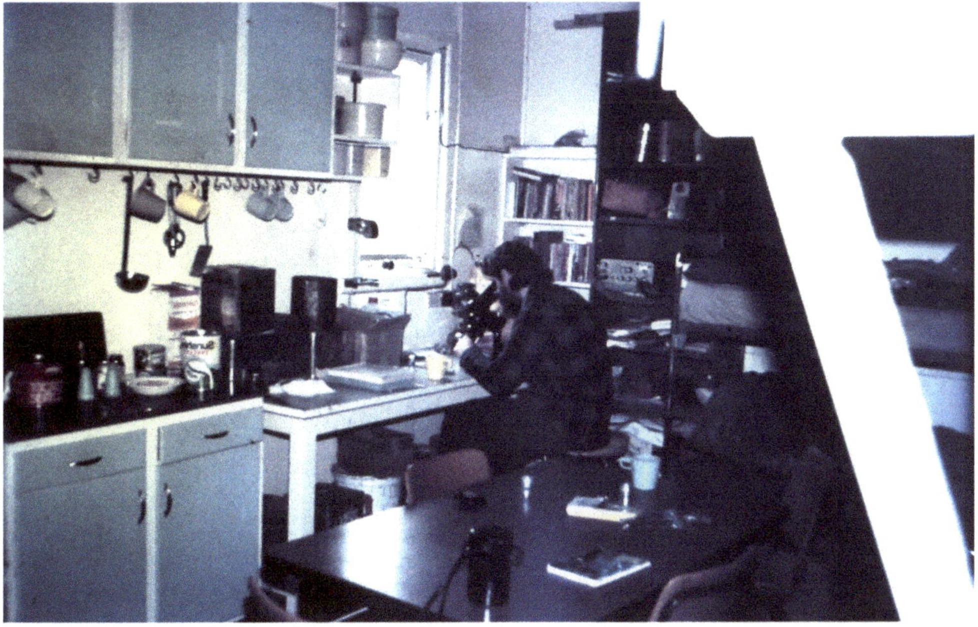

Above and below is the biologist, Geoff at work inside one of the island field huts, and the hot water heater creating some comforts of a home.

CHAPTER 4

MAJOR EVENTS

Both the RAAF Orion and Hercules did mail drops during the year to the island.

The mail drops landed mostly, directly on the orange circle marker in the middle of this picture by the RAAF Orion aircraft. When we received mail drops from the RAAF Hercules, it was more of a hit and miss affair as its accuracy in dropping the mail was not as good. Sometimes, some of the mail went out to sea, and never to be seen again.

Above two pictures show the target for the mail drop from the RAAF aircrafts. One dropped canister can be seen in the picture.

Above and below is the RAAF Orion aircraft coming in for a mail drop.

What an amazing aircraft this RAAF Orion is. Dropping mail, essential supplies, and parts, and of course some fresh fruit and vegetables. Even more so, what an amazing professional crew to do so with such accuracy.

An exciting event as the arrival of mail from our loved ones and family was sorely welcomed. Occasionally the mail would miss the narrow target on the isthmus and end out in the sea by the Hercules drop. Once a dinghy was launched to retrieve some of this mail, but this is a very rare accession as the surf is mostly treacherous and can only be done when the surf is calm. A rope was attached to the dinghy to the shore for safety. The Orion was amazingly accurate in delivering its payload right onto our ground target marked out in an orange plastic circle. The Orion though turbo prop, flew directly up into the clouds above us in a salute and returned home.

Dr David Lewis sailed to Antarctica and back single-handedly on his yacht, *'Ice Bird'*. A humble guy and an interesting adventurer, having his yacht rolled over by huge waves several times, in the horrific wild weather that the Southern Ocean can put on. He and the yacht barely survived. He visited Macquarie in my year on another trip, on his *'Ice Bird'* yacht. Pictured below, is David Lewis arriving at Macquarie Island. The radio operators did a great job bringing him in. The sea and island were fog-bound, which made it difficult for David to see the island. It took a couple of days for him to eventually find us. He was warmly welcomed to our station and its offerings of which we were sure he appreciated. His story is worth reading and can be retrieved from the reference located in Bibliology on the last page of this book.

Above is David Lewis arriving at the island, with his yacht *Ice Bird* in the background.

Courtesy of MAAS. Date unknown.

A horrid accident on the Island, January 1979. One of our biologists in the 1979 summer, was noticeably missing at lunchtime in the mess. He mentioned to one of our expeditioners, that he was going to North Head (next to the station) to study the birds perched high up on the cliff on the North side that morning. After some time, it was decided to go and look for him to make sure that he was ok. On the other side of the North Head hill, he was found at the bottom of the cliff fighting off the Skuas (a scavenger bird). He had multiple fractures and was in a bad way. We carried him back to the station's surgery on a stretcher through the dense Macquarie Island Cabbage plants, and up and around the North Head. The doctor examined him and called Head Office in Melbourne to get a ship down to pick him up immediately. The biologist's emotional and mental strength was strong, and he didn't complain about the pain or the condition he was in. I rigged up a communications link between the surgery and the Radio Hut for him to talk to his family over our radio network. This was done via the telephone system between the huts, then connected to the radio transmitter and receiver. There was a 24-hour watch put on him by the expeditioners, taking it in turn for his care. This required putting on hold various science projects, building projects and maintenance, but we managed and pulled together for the biologist. The *HMAS Hobart (II)* destroyer arrived almost at the same time as the *Thala Dan* five days later through rough seas and heavy weather. The biologist was transferred to the *HMAS Hobart (II)* via helicopter from the *Thala Dan*. The helicopter pilot flew the helicopter on the makeshift helipad, on the quarterdeck of the *HMAS Hobart (II)*, **while the ship was rolling in rough seas.** Some of these expeditioners are amazing and very brave, risking their lives for others! The biologist arrived in Tasmania was treated at the Royal Hobart Hospital, and then in Melbourne. He died a month after leaving the island from complications arising from spinal injuries, and an amputated leg. I returned to Australia several weeks later, at the end of the summer program. I heard from one of the expeditioners from this summer tragedy, saying that the 1979-year morale was down and depressive at times.

Above picture of North Head viewed from the station. The biologist fell off a cliff on the other side of North head while studying birdlife in the cliffs. January 1979.

After my return to Australia in February 1979, I returned to OTC (Aust.) Paddington (Sydney) International Switching & Testing Centre (ISTC). My section looked after the international telex network, and international radio circuits coming into and out of Sydney (Doonside Transmitter and Bringelly receiving stations). On the 28th of November, 1979 while I was there working in ISTC, disaster struck in Antarctica, at Mount Erebus on Ross Island. Information came into my section, that a sight-seeing plane Air New Zealand Flight 901 with 237 passengers and 20 crew crashed into Mount Erebus, killing all on board. Special radio circuits through OTC (Sydney) were set up to assist in the recovery of bodies and for the investigations of the tragedy.

CHAPTER 5

SOCIAL INTERACTION

The other 19 expeditioners in general, were terrific in their attitudes and professionalism and their trustworthiness. They exhibited a willingness to be part of a team in trying conditions of isolation, extreme weather, and to fulfil our obligations to the Antarctic Division and country. They had been selected as the best in their field from the many applicants, and selected for health, psychologically stable and suitable for wintering with others.

Our Station OIC was a highly ranked administrator as a Sports and Recreational officer, with the Australian government. He enjoyed getting involved and creating events with other expeditioners, as well as running the station efficiently.

40% of the expeditioners were married. Our female cook had her own female quarters in a separate building, built a year before to accommodate women expeditioners. The 1977 Station OIC and his doctor wife in the previous year, occupied these quarters, as well as a female radio operator. My own girlfriend and I decided not to wait for my return as 12 months wait was a long time. On return I met up with her and she wanted to get back together with me. After agreeing, she then told me that she was 3 months pregnant. It felt like to me, being hit with a large rock in the head. I am sure there were other stories of which I didn't hear about. What was good to see, was the wives who were waiting for their partners at the dock on return to the mainland. The Antarctic Division did supply us with 'Mrs Rob.' (Sheila Robinson), who handled personal things for us back home, kept in touch with the wives and family where necessary, and was well respected by expeditioners.

Minor accidents on the island consisted of an expeditioner attempting to inflate a tyre on the tractor in 1978, the tyre gave way and exploded, forcing up sand into the expeditioner's legs. The station doctor had to treat him for this injury. Other than a few injuries as such, the doctor mainly did research figures on all the expeditioners such as weigh gain/loss, food weighing, etc, and research on mice. It's generally a quiet year for the doctor, though a very important role to hold.

One expeditioner walked off the known track down the island and walked onto very soft and boggy feather bed and sunk up to his waist. Featherbed really stinks, due to centuries of decaying moss and mud under the featherbed. This was a stinky, mud and feathered experience not envied by anybody at the station.

The medical team on Macquarie consisted of a medical doctor, the Station OIC as the surgeon assistant, the Physicist as the anesthetist, the cook as the anesthetist assistant (both having a short stint in an Australian hospital operating room). The doctor had a short course in dentistry as well. One did not want to get sick!

Besides taking it in turns to cook every Sunday, there were duties for the week by each expeditioner in turn. Usually by the one whose turn it was to cook on the Sunday. This consisted of mopping the mess floor every day, helping in the kitchen, setting the tables, and putting out the food during mealtimes. We also took turns in the station on a weekly night fire watch. Should there be a fire on the station, valuable buildings and assets would be gone and operations severely curtailed.

Everyone on the station must take it in turn to cook on Sundays for the other expeditioners. This allows the cook to have time out one day a week. I remembered the cook also getting time out to explore the island and the wildlife for a week or so. She deserved it. It was amazing, what she was able to come up with using frozen food and tins of food, to present us with hearty meals during the day. We helped ourselves to a hot breakfast, to get us going in the morning. The cook was able to have several hours off in the morning to do her own thing. From lunch time onwards, it was busy for her until the evening meal. After work, we would likely be at the bar in the mess, drinking our home-made beer, just chilling out, as most of us worked very hard during the day. Often in the harsh outdoor environment. We worked long hours in the summer, whereas in the winter, it was less. In our free time, of which we had little during the summer, there was an excellent library, a HiFi system to listen to our favourite music, darts, and a billiard table. A piano in the small hut across from the mess if one could play it. Two nights a week we had 'movie night'. This consisted of a reel-to-reel projector, screen, and classic old reel movies collected over the years to watch. We were disappointed when watching a movie called 'The World of Suzie Wong'. The ending was missing from the end of the film. So, we were very disappointed not knowing what happened to this young, gorgeous-looking Asian lady. It wasn't until 2021, that I came across the movie and saw the final ending of this story. There was also a VHS video cassette player with a cathode ray tube style television. Photography was the major attraction, with a dark room to develop our black and white film, and colour film, and prints which were black and white or colour. Cibachrome photographic paper was a common colour medium that we used. Most photographic chemicals were supplied by the Antarctic Division, for official and personal use.

We were given the home brew ingredients from the well-known Carlton and United Brewery. This involved in making up a vat with yeast and the specially supplied ingredients. When the vat of beer was ready to be siphoned out into bottles, one would have to suck on the tube to get the beer out of the vat into the bottle. Hereby taking a mouthful of beer with every bottle filled and having to swallow each time. By the end of the night brewing session, one was rather tipsy, but it was worth it, as the home brew was a nice drop to be had. One good thing about chilling the beer, just leave it outside for 30 minutes.

Above is Brendon (diesel mechanic) and Phil (Station OIC) enjoying a home-made beer.

Above, I enjoyed a beer also.

For the brave at heart, there was a sauna and freezing cold tub of water outside.

Above is a picture of the billiard table in the mess room. Des was hamming It up when I took the photo.

In the middle of winter when there was little daylight, I felt creative and carved an abstract woman figurine out of Canadian Red Cedar and put it behind the bar.

Mid-winter celebrations were and are always a highlight for expeditioners of any year wintering on the research stations, or with the ANARE Club mid-winters dinners back home. Dinner was a formal dress affair, with the most elaborate food kept especially for this occasion. The usual ANARE play 'Cinderella' was performed by some of the expeditioners. No need to say what the characters looked like in the performance. Hilarious and fun for us all. Other plays were written and performed as well by the expeditioners for this special day.

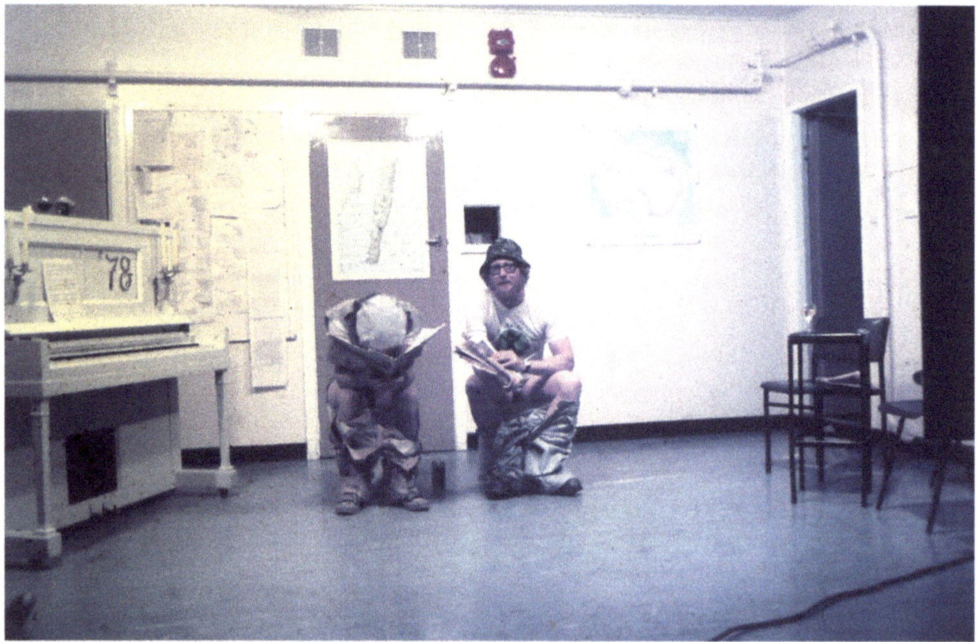

Above two pictures are plays written and performed by our expeditioners.

Above author after the traditional Mid Winters swim.

Above, and from left to right: The author, the Station OIC (Phil), radio operator (Noddy), and the doctor (Des). It felt like hitting a brick wall when I dived into the surf, as the temperature was only 5 degrees Celsius. It felt warm once out of the water, but this air temp was only about the same as the surf.

Mid winter's traditional swim in the island's bay, was initiated by Sir Douglas Mawson, when he dived overboard from his first voyage to the Antarctica continent, at Commonwealth Bay about 1911. Legend has it, that he dived in to retrieve a box that had fallen into the bay, thought to be valuable. Apparently, it wasn't. But this started the midwinter swim tradition by the ANARE expeditioners on all the research stations since.

The monotony of the station life was broken by some-one's birthday, where dinner would be a little more special, and the wine and a creative birthday cake would come out to the tables.

I managed to form a jazz duet with the doctor who played piano and knew the old jazz numbers, and I played the trumpet. I had the jazz music scores for piano and trumpet. Soon we found someone who could make and play a set of drums, a singer, a tea box base player, and a banjo player. We had a full-on swing jazz band! The band entertainment was performing several times during the year, until early mornings. Playing until 6.00am in the morning sometimes, and most slept in until late Sunday morning with almost no-one attending breakfast. It was so much fun. I noticed that most of the records played on the HI FI system in the mess, were mainly male singers and rock bands of this the 70s era. The guys were jovial and talking loudly as happens in male groups. I put on a woman singer recording, and I noticed the effect on the guys, quietening the night events.

Although the above photo was double exposed through a camera fault, it is possible to see myself playing the trumpet with the doctor on piano.

The doctor was a bit of character and well experienced in his many trips to the continent and wintering on various Australian Antarctic Stations. He wore shorts wherever possible until he ventured to the plateau to walk down the island. It was obviously too cold and the exposure too severe away from the station. He would then change into long trousers. Being an expeditioner is a levelling experience. Everyone is as important as the next on the station. The pace of life is slower than back at home as well.

Above shows us outside the mess on the station. Would you believe it, the sun is out! So, let's have a barbeque! 1978.

Macquarie Island folk band performing in the summer of 1979.

Above, volley ball was a favourite inside the storage building.

Above, VHS video tapes and television showed many, in the 1970s, modern movies.

Above three pictures are some of our forms of entertainment 1978 winter and 1979 summer.

Above enjoying listening to vinyl records.

Above shows a favourite past time is developing and organising film and photos that has been developed in the station photographic room by the expeditioners in their spare time.

Above is a special curry night in the storeroom.

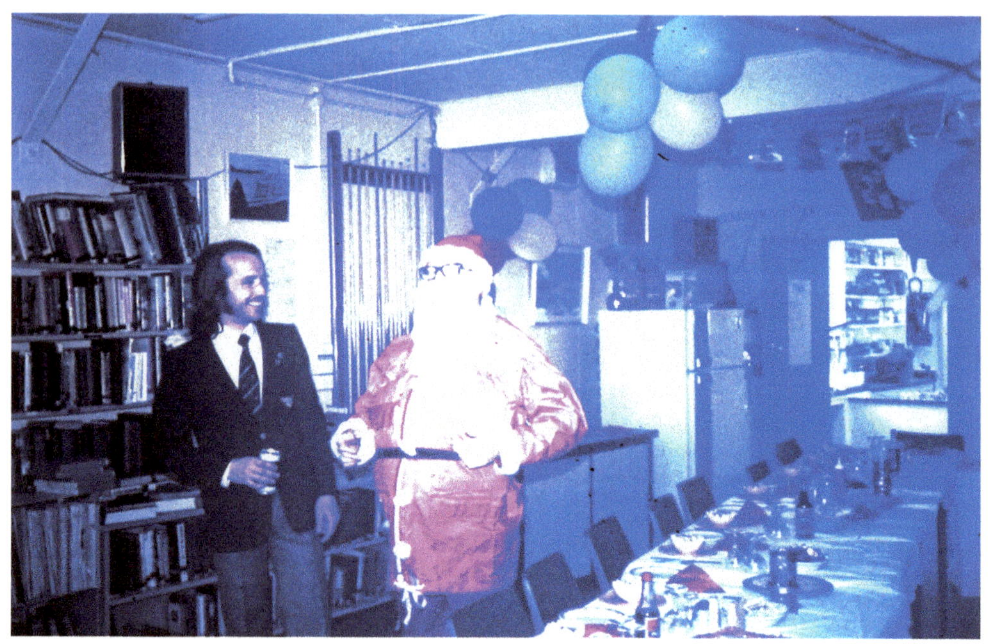

Above two pictures, show that Christmas was a special occasion for us, being without our families and friends back home. We decided to make each other a present. Some were amazingly creative and a memoir to take home.

Above is one of the creations made by our cook, Enid.

Above is Enid, our female cook on Macquarie Island, 1978.

A feast for the special time of Christmas '78 & '79 to be had. The cook/chef and the helpers make a wonderful spread for us, and memories.

Above is the chef from 1979 putting on a spread for a special occasion.

Besides all the seriousness, there were fun time made by the expeditioners. Like a golf tournament, and creative antics. Not only were the expeditioners the tops in their trades and science professions, but they were also innovators of antics.

Above two pictures show a golf tornament underway in 1979.

Above is myself with Laurie our Physicist, in the middle of winter, 1978

Above are the 1979 summer expeditioners enjoying time out.

Above are the 1978 winterers also enjoying time out after work at the bar, the bar being previously modified by the carpenters in 1978.

Time out was much needed by the guys at times. As we worked hard, especially being outside for several of us, and missing our families and partners and friends also. These pictures describe again what 'time out' was like on the island.

Our cans of beer were rationed, so they were kept for special occasions such as a get together in the donga after work.

Two expeditioners, Brendon and George hamming it up on the dance floor.

Camping was no joy though! I spent one-night camping on the plateau with the doctor and plumber. I could put up with the howling winds and the dampness of the tent and drizzle, but my failure was that I couldn't sleep through the snoring of one of our parties. From then on, I stayed in the field huts around the island and was quite happy to have a 300-metre climb instead, every morning to the plateau, after a good night's sleep.

Above is a picture of myself, the doctor, and the plumber on the right, about to start out on this trip down the island.

Above is me and the Laurie ready to trek down the island. I found the gum boots was more suitable for me than the ANARE boots, as much of the island tracks were wet and soggy, and I would take the gum boot off easily to tip out the water if necessary.

Above three pictures are some of the island treks that I did. Which were for 10 days, 5 each time during the 15 months of my stay (Total of 50 days down the island). Geoff, the biologist, stayed down the island most of the year of 1978, living in 6 field huts available at the time, for his research.

Three months before the supply ship (*Nella Dan*) was to come and pick up our 1978 wintering expeditioners, there was a feeling that the end of our stay was approaching and eagerness to return to our roots in Australia was starting to be felt. On the final night celebrations, our Station OIC invited the new 1979 expeditioners to join us for dinner, and to enjoy our jazz band to early morning. It was strange that not many of both wintering years stayed until late. I often wondered if the fun just wasn't there as the outgoing expeditioners were leaving the next day, and the incoming weren't in tune or accepting of celebrating the way we did. A whole bag of mixed feelings that night, I think. We 1978 expeditioners must have looked a sight to the incoming expeditioners. Our clothes were worn, and dirty outdoor weather ventiles in appearance. Compared to the incoming expeditioners, wearing their bright and clean Macquarie weather gear. Many were new to this new lifestyle, I thought, as we were 12 months before.

The 1979 chef, Alan, was a very experienced chef, keeping the expeditioners happy with his various food creations.

Above is Alan in the kitchen.

I stayed on for another summer in 1979 with this new crew. Seeing the 1978 expeditioners leave was like mixed emotions, as it signified the end of a trying year work wise in radio and a new crew to know. The 1979 expeditioners treated me well and I enjoyed the summer until tragedy happened with their biologist.

I also did not know that the property boom had started in Sydney, and I would be way behind in my extra earnings from my 3 months extra summer stay, compared to the increases of properties during this period. I did manage though to buy a 100-year-old plus 4-bedroom terrace house in Alexandria, Sydney on return to Australia.

Above two pictures are of the 1978 expeditioners leaving, to be taken back to Australia on the *Nella Dan*.

Leaving the island (in the summer of 1979) and 1979 expeditioners was again mixed bag of emotions. I witnessed the grieving of some of the expeditioners from the loss one of their mates (biologist). I felt for them and wondered what the wintering was going to be like for them. I was pleased to finally go home aboard the *Thala Dan*. 15 months was a long time away from home.

I boarded the ship *Thala Dan* after she serviced the other Australian Science Research Stations in Antarctica. Seeing Australia for the first time in 15 months was going to be an unknown, as I had changed and where would my life take me to now. I returned to The Overseas Telecommunications Commission exchange in Paddington, Sydney and a year later, my desire to return to the Antarctic Division brought about my new adventure to the Antarctic continent. Casey Station 1981.

Above are the summer 1979 expeditioners boarding the ship. It was a hazardous affair for the Army LARC, with strong coastal ocean swells making the boarding difficult and dangerous.

And would you believe it, the ocean was a smooth as glass, all the way back to Melbourne on the *Thala Dan*.

Sailing on the way back, an announcement over the PA system, calling my name to go to the ship's radio room and speak to the ship's radio operator. I was told and found that the ship's radio transmitter power supply located outside within a small hatch of the ship had gone up in smoke. "Great", I thought, knowing I would be sitting on the hatchway, for hours rewiring the power supply with the sea spray against my back, and rolling back and forth in the ocean swell. When I finished the repairs, the ships radio operator gave me the thumbs up, and communications back to Australia and Denmark resumed.

Approaching the Australian mainland, I could smell the burnt summer air which I no longer take for granted.

Above, onboard the *Thala Dan*, February 1979, approaching Melbourne.

Above the on-ship helicopters are taken back to the mainland after doing vital work in Antarctica. These helicopters will be mentioned later in the book during my time at Casey Station 1981.

Only just off the *Thala Dan*, it was a welcomed sight to see my parents waiting on the dock for me. My parents thought I'd be lonely while away, but to their surprise, I had my arms around the young female ornithologist when we docked in Melbourne. My father's instruction to me, was to cut my hair and shave off my beard.

I jumped into a car to take me to the Antarctic Divisions H.O, to get debriefed. To my surprise, I was doing 80km/hr, and it was frightening. I slid down in my seat and closed my eyes for a while wishing I was doing 5km/hr like on Macquarie for the last 15 months. Once in H.O., I noticed straight away the stress levels were very high in everyone, including those I met elsewhere during the week. A week later I saw no more stress levels in anyone, as I was there also.

Above on the *Thala Dan,* arriving in Melbourne port, ready to disembark and to be debriefed at the Antarctic Division. Parents were waiting on the dock. The ornithologist and me. February 1979.

On my arrival in Melbourne, I learnt that my cousin Jennine had leukaemia and had been in and out of hospital for years. Missing school, outings with friends, boyfriends, etc. Everything an 18-year-old girl would be doing. My immediate thought was to take her elsewhere other than Melbourne and experience life somewhere else on a holiday. I suggested to her that Hobart, Tasmania would be a great place to go and explore. She and her parents agreed. So, we flew out and stayed at the Hobart Casino for the week. We visited the usual touristy spots in Hobart and noted that Hobart was quite a cultural city with a lot of history. I hired a car, and we went north up the island, to see Tony, who I'd just wintered with on Macquarie (1978), our 2nd carpenter, who had a house on a communal farm. The houses surrounding the common farmland, were all built from stones and Jennine was surprised with the lovely architecture and communal farm idea. Arrival back to the Hobart Casino, saw Jennine fall ill and in much pain in the middle of the night. I called the doctor immediately and he came to the hotel room. His comment was after Jennine asked for the usual morphine injection that she receives back home, was that "she could just be a drug addict and that he couldn't give any". Jennine was in excruciating pain and tears running down her face. By morning, Jennine recovered for the time being. We flew back home to her family, and I flew to Brisbane to see my family. Jennine died two weeks later.

Back to normal life: After taking leave from the Antarctic Division, in Brisbane, and with a haircut and shave, I returned to O.T.C. in Sydney and commenced duties in the O.T.C. International Exchange in Paddington, from where I came from briefly before my adventures on Macquarie Island. My first port of call in Sydney was the jazz venue at The Vanity Fair in the city, where my jazz friends hang out. Someone bought me a beer and continued as though I had not been away for 18 months. How nice. Our friendships had sustainability.

Macquarie Island expeditioners - 1978

1st Row — NEIL McARTHUR (MET),ALAN WINTER (CHEF),KEVIN WAKE-DYSTER (GEO),PETER DEDDON (MET).
2nd Row — PETER MENTHA (PLUMBER),MARK DURRE' (UAP),ROB COOPER (ELECTRICAL),BRIAN HARVEY (DIESO);
2nd Row — JOHN TRETHEWEY (RAD TECH),NIGEL BROTHERS (BIOLOGIST),ROB CROMBIE (CARPENTER).
3rd Row — ROD HUTCHINSON (MET),JOHN FLANNERY (MET TECH),IVAN HAWTHORN (OIC),JOHN STALKER (MET OIC);
3rd Row — BILL PRITCHARD (RAD SUP),PETER KING (RAD),PETER BANNISTER (MET),JOHN BELL (DOC).

Macquarie Island expeditioners - 1979

CHAPTER 6

MACQUARIE ISLAND WILDLIFE

Hurd Point is home to the largest royal penguin colony in the world. It has over 180,000 breeding pairs of birds during summer. Gentoo penguins, King penguins, and southern elephant seals can be observed from the field hut. The hut can be seen in the foreground. Climbing up towards the top of this cliff, Light Mantle Albatross on nests can be observed close. It means that as you are holding onto the Tussock Grass on the cliff face, the mother and chick are literally less than 300mm away from your face. The chicks generally to protect themselves, do so by regurgitating their fish food at you, and you stink for the rest of your stay down the island because of this. Luckily, I witnessed the mother look at me as no threat, and gently lowered her beak, pushing the chick under her to protect myself from the chick regurgitating onto me. Animals are amazingly intelligent and understanding of their environments, and people at times. People are not a threat to the birds on the island. For example, later in this book, will be a photo of myself squatting next to a Wandering Albatross. The Wandering Albatross allowed me to pat it and put my hand inside of her feathers. I found that she had a small body as my hand went all the way in up to my wrist. Beautiful.

The above two pictures are of Hurd Point. A breeding ground of 180,000 pairs of penguins. 1978.

The island was prolific with wildlife. Millions of penguins of various types, various types of seals including a prolific amount of Elephant seals with the bulls having harems, and capable of mating with a cow for a week at a time (phew). Albatrosses of various types, and other birds (Skuas) necessary to prevent disease from forming from dead animals by devouring the carcasses. And of course, the introduced animals and vermin those that were classified as pests, and that were destroying the wildlife and vegetation and the fragile terrain.

The courting of penguins: A single male penguin would find a vacant piece of beach and make a nest out of pebbles. He would then put his beak in the air and make a cry. Not long later, a single female penguin would be at his side. The courting would begin, with both penguins bowing and raising their heads in unison. Then they would mate. The same pair of penguins would then mate for life, coming back to the exact position on the beach each year. The female would go out into the ocean to find food and bring it back to the nest. The male penguin would keep the egg on its feet, squatting to keep it warm and incubate it, until the egg hatched. The pair would watch over the chick until it loses its 'down' and would be able to then swim out into the ocean at the end of summer. All these penguins would then spend the winter out in the ocean until the next summer comes around. The cycle would then repeat. The parent penguins would mate for life!

Penguin rookery.

King penguin rookery. Chicks still covered in 'down'.

King penguins returning from the ocean, looking for food for their chicks.

Above show a Royal penguin with an egg on its nest.

Royal penguin rookery.

Gentoo penguin and chick.

A rare Chinstrap penguin to the island.

Wandering Albatross sitting on an egg.

Wandering Albatross on nest and egg located in the tussock grass.

Above show a Cormorant pair nesting.

Above is a Weka in the tussock grass in the station grounds.

Bird eggs on the ground. Proned to vermin or cats eating them.

Above are Elephant seals.

Above are Elephant seals playing.

Above is rare to the island, Leopard seal on the beach.

Above is a male Elephant seal (Bull) with probiscis to show the cows he is ready to mate this summer.

Above is an Elephant seal harem. A very smelly place to be.

Above is a 3-month-old Elephant seal.

During the summer breeding season, many baby Elephant seals are accidentally crushed by the bull Elephant seals. Bull Elephant seals can weigh up to 3 tonnes , and the baby seals must keep out of their way to survive.

Above is a Male Hooker's Sea Lion.

Above Skuas devour carcasses, thereby keeping the diseases down amongst the other animals. One nearly picked out my eye when I rested on the plateau and had a quick nap. I woke up just in time.

Above, cats to be eventually eradicated from the island.

Above two Fur seals in the coastal rocks.

CHAPTER 7

MACQUARIE ISLAND "BLACK & WHITE"

Above picture show us just prior to trekking down the island, with the doctor and the plumber and me. Macquarie Island 1978.

Above we are camping somewhere down the island on the plateau. Conditions were wet and windy as Macquarie Island is at most of the time.

Above is the doctor and the author pictured in one of the island field huts. Also, with us was the station plumber, taking this picture.

Above is one of the island's field huts that I stayed at for the night.

Above two pictures are of the "Light Mantle Albatross' with its chick near the top of the cliff, Hurd Point.

Above is the author heading down to the field hut located in one of the many bays around the island.

Above is the author doing some photography down the island somewhere.

Above are the sealers digesters used for boiling down the penguins and seals for their valuable oil.

Above is an expeditioner who didn't make it home. He died when he broke through the surface ice of the nearby lake, skiing, 1948.

To be Buried on Macquarie Island

MELBOURNE, Sunday — Senior meteorologist of the Australian research party on Macquarie Island, Mr. John Windsor, who died on Friday after an operation for acute appendicitis, will be buried on the island.

Because there is no padre on the island, his widow, Mrs. J. G. Windsor, of Pascoe Vale, has agreed to let his team mates take charge of the funeral arrangements.

Mr. Windsor will be buried near the grave of Mr. Charles Scoble, the engineer who was drowned while ski-ing in 1948.

No other meteorologist will be sent to the island, because landing hazards are too great, and the whole party is to return in April.

Courtesy of Trove. Date unknown

Above are the remains of a previous year radio mast or gantry (located on the top of North Head).

Above picture is me getting up close and personal with a young female Elephant seal.

Above is a female Elephant seal a bit too close.

Above picture is of a picture of a Giant Petrel and her chick.

Above picture is me with a Wandering Albatross on her nest, high up on the island plateau. Completely unafraid of humans.

Above picture is of a male Gentoo penguin calling out to attract a female mate. Note that he has already built his nest out of pebbles from the beach.

Above are King penguin chicks, still with down

Above is a picture of a Macquarie Island bird that makes its nest in the soft ground, by making a hole in the soft ground. Picture shown with a biologist.

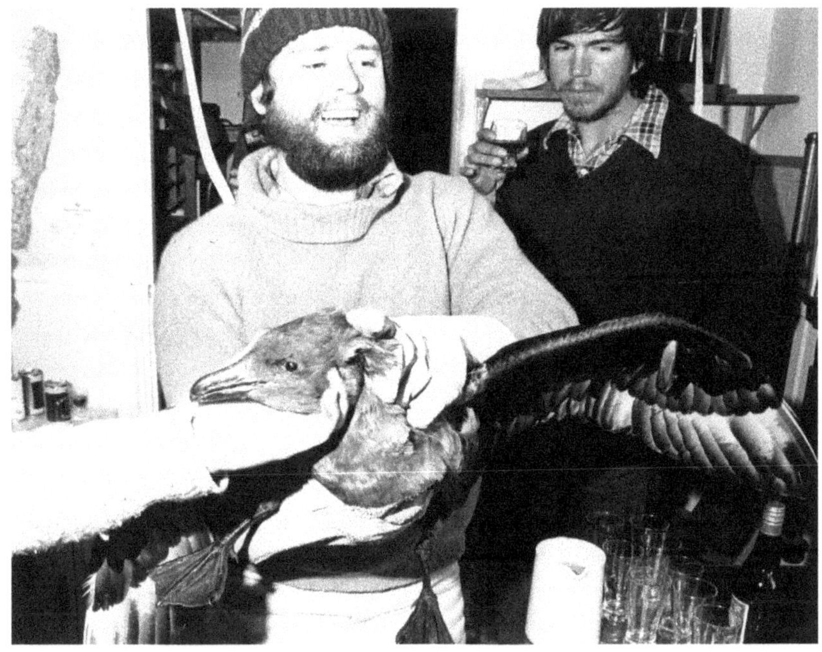

Above is a skua that made the mistake of flying into the Met observer's office. It was caught and released outside.

Above is the Macquarie Island mid-winter dinner menu.

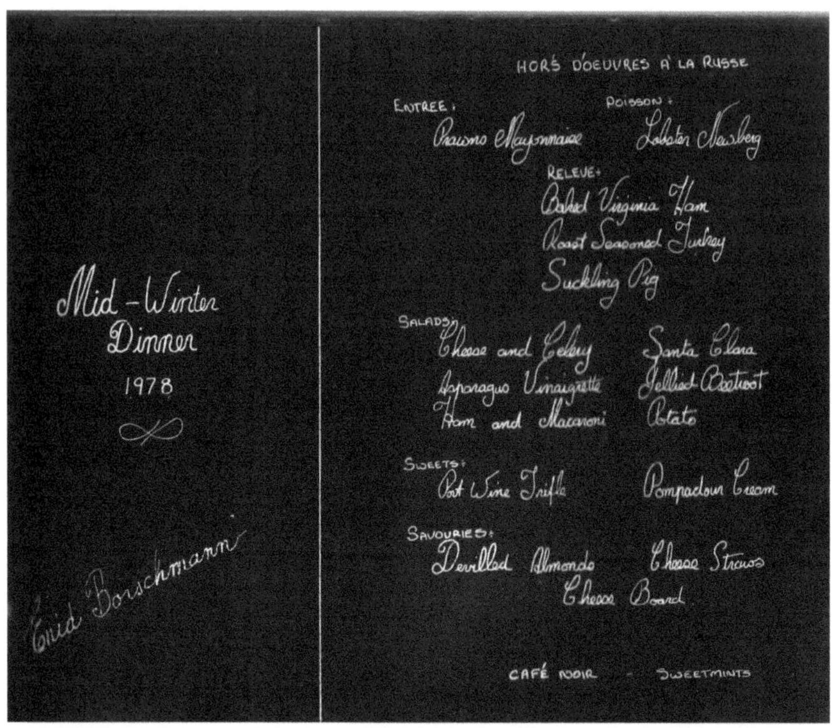

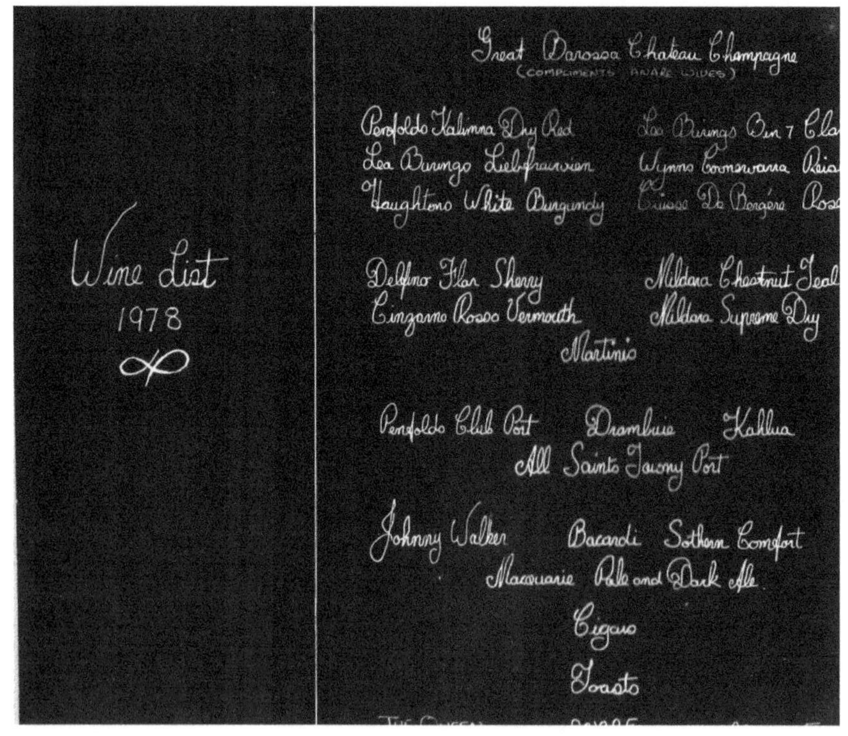

We didn't exactly starve!

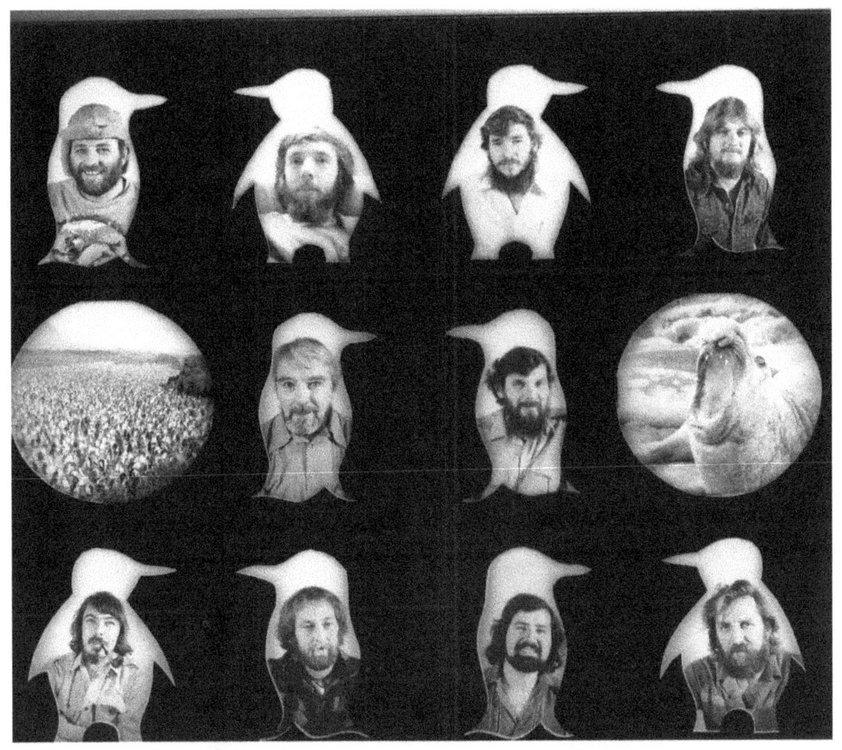

Pick out the author? Clue: He has a beard!

131

Above two pictures: Yes, that's me atop of the radio mast putting the antenna wires back on, after howling winds the day before brought them down. This mast was to be replaced during the '79 summer. The reason was due to heavy corrosion mid-way up.

Above show Macquarie Island in bad weather. The one of two streetlights at the time.

Above I found a break in the signal cable halfway to the Transmitter Hut, causing the transmitter to intermittently turn off and on randomly.

Above is a cave on the island where the stranded sealers may have refuge in the 19th or 20th century. There, I am holding weathered old bones from a Wandering Albatross, presumably eaten by the sealers.

Above: Here I am in my donga, reading about Michelangelo's life story. 'The Agony and the Ecstasy'. A bit like being here on the island.

Above two pictures are of myself helping to provide entertainment for the expeditioners, usually on a Saturday night. This being our Macquarie Island Jazz Band, '78ers.

Above picture show that football was a favourite pastime for the '79ers

Above picture shows the '79 doctor trying to co-ordinate the expeditioners to simulate the pistons in a diesel engine. Not an easy task.

Above self-entertainment, showing that dance partners that could dance, were a scarcity on the island.

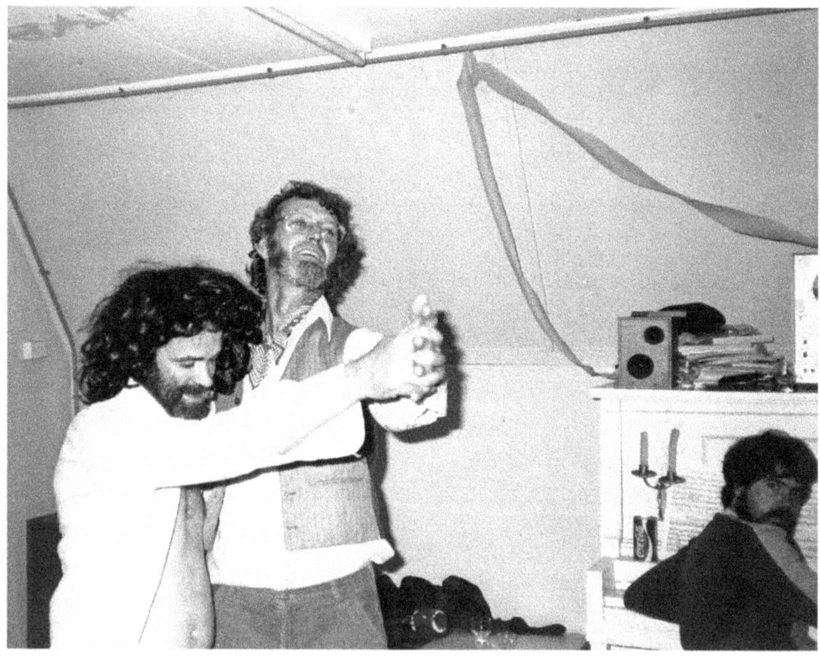

Above showing the '79 doctor and carpenter doing the tango, or sort of. With the radio tech. playing the piano, sort of.

Above surfing was easier, back in Australia that is.

Above '79er's Jazz Band. Let's do some original Macquarie Island music.

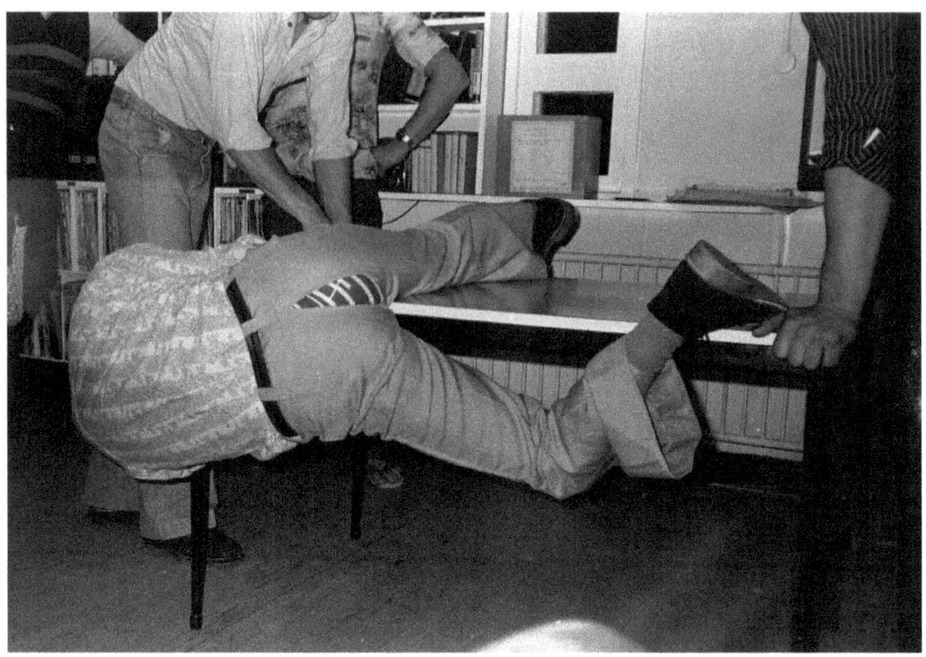

Above challenge. Who can go around a tabletop without touching the floor? One expeditioner managed to do so. Although he brought us to stitches as he needed a few himself!

Above is the mess where we dined and entertained ourselves.

Above is my first social interaction with a young female in 12 months. Summer of 1979.

Above describes a Christmas sleigh ride around the station. The Met balloon shed and Met office in the background.

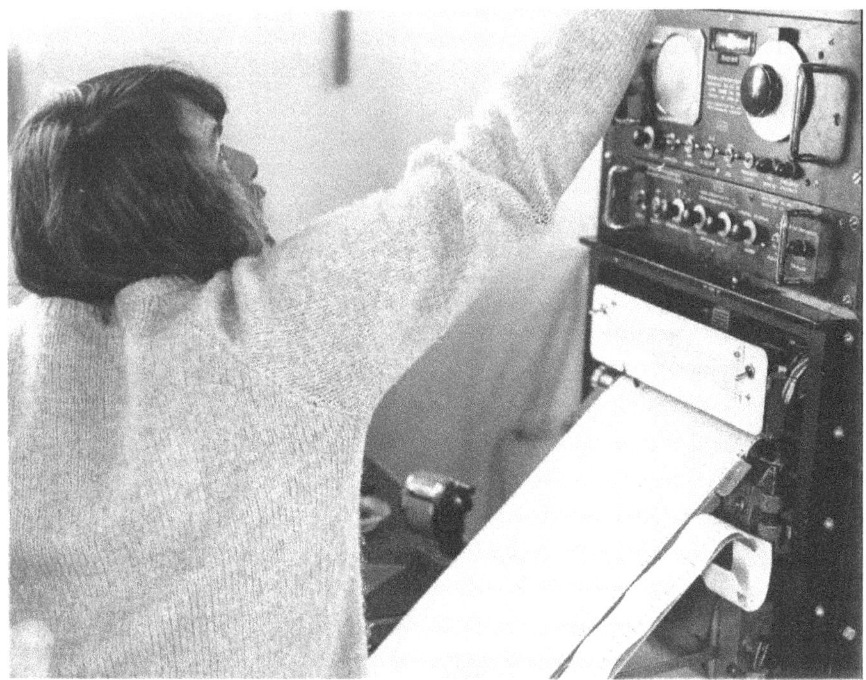

Above shows the 1979 Met Observer recording weather information from a released balloon. Its position is also tracked by a weather balloon radar.

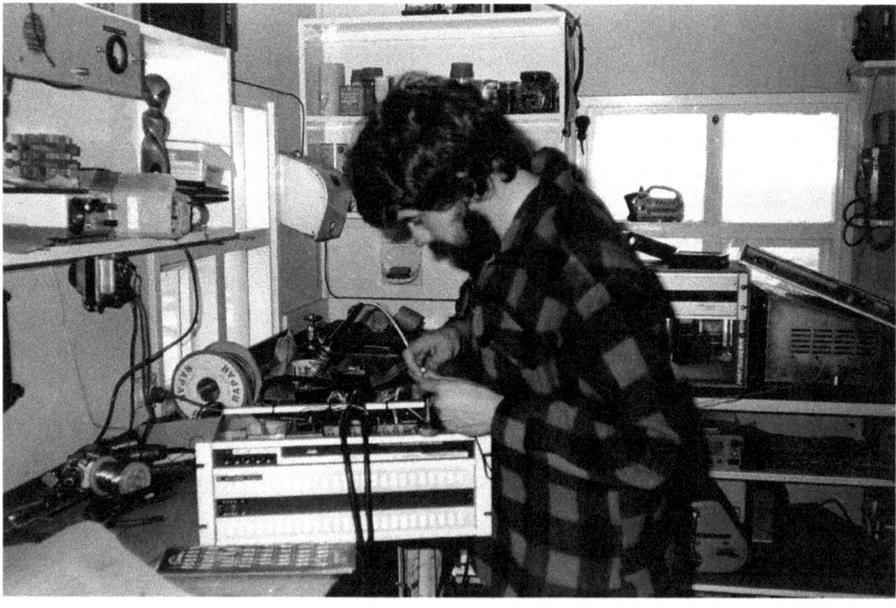

Above is the incoming '79 Radio Tech (Radio OIC). setting up a new telex electronic storage unit in the radio workshop, located in the Radio Hut itself.

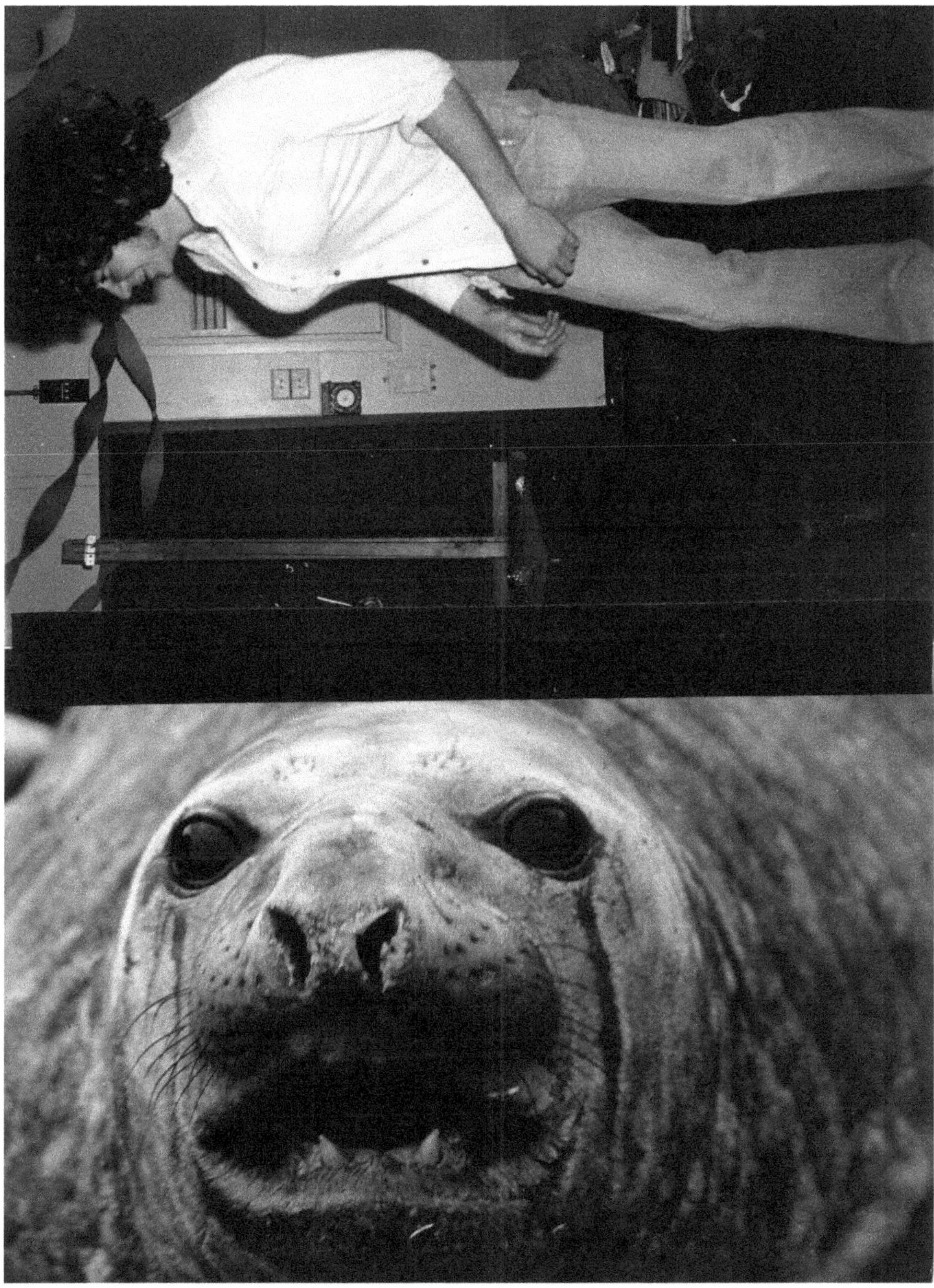

Above one of the expeditioners created the 'Animal and Tart' party dinner menu cover above, and on the next page, inside of the menu.

THE "ANIMAL & TART" MENU

SUMMERERS' SPECIAL
CHEF: Specially imported from the "Great South"
The best available

HORS D'OEUVRES:
LOCAL LIMPETS (FRESH FROM THE ROCKS)

SOUP:
SEAL WALLOW SOUP
STOMACH PUMP SOUP

MAIN COURSE:
SWEET & SOUR WEKA
ROAST PENGUIN A LA MACQUARIE ISLAND
BRAISED BABY SEAL STEAK
FISH (LOCAL VARIETY - WITH WORMS)

DESSERT:
APRICOT PIE A LA HURD POINT
APPLE SCREE SLOPE
} WITH PENGUIN POO OR CORMORANT CRAP

COFFEE (POSSIBLY TEA - IF SPECIALLY REQUESTED)

WINE LIST
EXTENSIVE

ENTERTAINMENT: THE STRUMPET

WHAT EVER YOU DO ALL THIS YEAR:
REMEMBER THE RECIPES FOR A

VERY HAPPY YEAR

Another very palatable repast.

Above is a penguin in trouble. Pictured with the station's carpenter, 1979.

Above are King penguins curiously pecking at my boots.

Above are two Fur seals near the station, with Kelp in the background.

Above is typical rough surf along the coastline. This photo is taken next to the station.

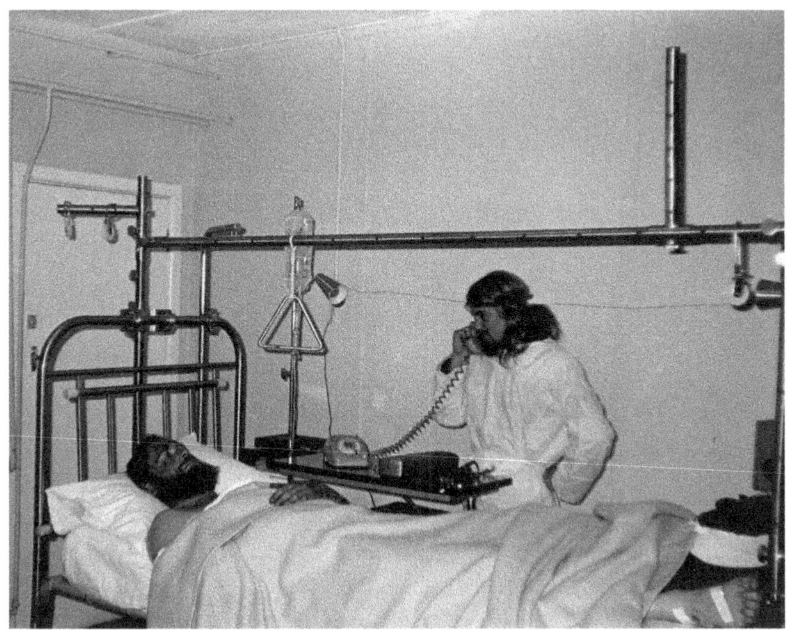

Above is the injured biologist in the surgery. Myself testing the telephone line that I installed to the Radio Hut. The biologist was able to talk to his family from then on. January 1979.

Above are the '79ers carrying the biologist to the helicopter, to be lifted out to the *HMAS Hobart (II)*.

Above, the helicopter coming in to airlift the injured biologist out to the *HMAS Hobart (II)*. The helicopter was from the *Thala Dan*. Both ships arrived roughly at the same time after enduring rough seas and weather.

Above, the helicopter pilot is one of the bravest expeditioners I've met during my two winters with ANARE. He flew the injured biologist to the *HMAS Hobart (II)*. This pilot flew his helicopter **on the rear deck** of the destroyer, whilst the ship rolled in heavy ocean swells, and the biologist was lifted out of the helicopter. Both ships can be seen in the background.

Above are the '79ers putting the biologist into the helicopter.

Above two photos are of the *HMAS Hobart (II)* and the *Thala Dan* arriving at the same time after 5 days sailing though gruelling weather to be at the island. The *Thala Dan* had a helicopter on board, which took the biologist to the deck of the *HMAS Hobart (II)*. Then to speed the injured biologist to the Royal Hobart Hospital, and then later to be transferred to a Melbourne hospital.

CHAPTER 8

THE AUSTRALIAN ANTARCTIC DIVISION
(CASEY STATION 1981 - 12 months)

Courtesy of The Mercury

The reason for going again, as you can see, Macquarie Island whet my appetite for further adventures. It must be in my Nordic blood, to travel and experience life. So, as I was still young and single, Antarctica was on my list as I love the cold. Up to the age of 38 years, I continued to do interesting things and hold interesting technical positions in communications and electronics. My career path was expanded from the Overseas Telecommunications Commission Coastal Radio Station Darwin, the International Telex Exchange in Paddington Sydney, Norwegian North Sea Oil in instrumentation on oil rigs and on shore, Site Manager for the installation of the Australian National Earth Satellite Stations (AUSSAT), Perth and Darwin and Brisbane Stations. Later the same for TVW-7 in Perth and Ten-10 in Sydney with another company, Sydney Opera House as eventual supervisor in the Electronics Department, and at the same time I was the founder of the employment agency "Nannies & Helper P/L" in Sydney which is still running successfully today. When I reached 38 years old, I wanted to settle down with a doctor from Chile, but disaster struck with my health. It has been resolved since and I eventually married a Brisbane lady and helped raise her daughter in Brisbane. My two sisters and parents also lived in Brisbane.

I think Macquarie Island 1978/79 was an exceptional time, with the building program, the arrival of the yacht 'Ice Bird' with Dr. David Lewis the intrepid sailor and researcher, the death of one of our expeditioners, mail drops by the RAAF, and my own challenge to bring the station radio equipment, antennae, masts to a reliable operational state before leaving the island. My strong belief is to have a positive impact no matter where I went in my professional or personal life.

I resigned from The Overseas Telecommunications Commission (Aust) in 1980 and joined again with The Department of Science and Technology (Antarctic Division). This time the Division wanted me to serve at the Casey Research Station in Antarctica, on the continent, below Perth. The Radio OIC position was taken by an ABC Television Senior Technical Officer (Herman) from Hobart, Tasmania. My position was under his, likely due to his more senior position in the ABC and age. We got along well. This time I was 27 years of age, with a lot of communications and radio experience. There was an exciting time to be had at Casey I felt at the time, though yet to experience working in such a severe, icy, cold, environment.

Above are two pictures of the present Australian Antarctic Division buildings (2018), headquarters no longer in Melbourne as it was when I went south, but now located at Kingston (near Hobart), Tasmania.

Training consisted of survival training at the Snowy Mountains, Telex machine maintenance in Melbourne, 10KW transmitter maintenance training at the Laverton RAAF base, near Melbourne, as well as mandatory psychology and medical tests. Live fire fighting training was a necessary requirement for the expeditioners on all stations.

I was seen off by family, this time by my cousin Deb and aunty Ethyl from the Melbourne docks, aboard the *Thala Dan*. This time we met high swells on the ocean on the way to Casey which took over 10 days to reach. Approximately 3,842km sailing from Melbourne to Casey Station. The *Thala Dan* sails like a corkscrew in the ocean, due to way she is built and loaded with cargo. It is impossible not to fall into the corridor bulkhead constantly while trying to get from one cabin to another. As one's foot cannot know how the ship is going to lurch during the voyage. The Southern Ocean is an experience to behold.

Above is somewhere just out from Melbourne on the way to Casey Station. The Southern Ocean has yet to be experienced.

Above three photos are of our first signs of icebergs. Meaning Casey was only a couple of days away.

Above is our first signs of wildlife (seals) in Antarctic waters. Our initial welcoming party.

Above, we eventually reached calmer ocean waters near Antarctica after experiencing the horrendous Southern Ocean swells. I could then see a defined line of ice in front of us, going from left and to the right of us, all the way to the horizon.

Above two photos: From here the helicopter was launched, and now no longer had a free ride. The pilot's job was to find a safe path through the thickening sea ice and icebergs all the way to Casey Station for the ship to sail through. This sea ice can extend several hundred kilometres out from Casey during the early summer.

CHAPTER 9

ARRIVAL AT CASEY STATION - 1981

On arrival at Casey Station, we were greeted with the customary explosion of old diesel stored in drums near the foreshore, away from any buildings. The 1980 expeditioners gave us a great welcome this way as we sailed into the bay. I think they were pleased to see us. They had just completed 12 months there in isolation, extreme weather conditions, and a barren environment. One of the expeditioners there commented that he really wanted to see greenery again.

Above two photos: It was now our turn, the 1981ers to get ashore and start unloading food and material supplies. This time the bay waters were calmer and made it easier to unload for the Army LARCs, compared to Macquarie Island in 1978.

Above three photos show that a barge was required for large and heavy vehicles and containers.

Above picture shows the *Thala Dan* just outside of Casey Station near one of many islands in the bay.

Above two photos of the *Thala Dan* at Casey Station. 1981.

Above is Casey Station 1981. Plans were to replace these buildings with those being constructed further up the limited rocky landscape, as shown in the below picture.

Above is the unloading of building material at the new building site, for the continuation of the new Casey Station building project.

This old Casey Station in which our expeditioners worked in until 1988, has now been completely replaced with many similar above and below coloured insulated buildings.

Above on the left are the yellow and blue buildings, on the location of the new Casey site under construction. Casey Station is at the upper mid right side of the picture, and the old, abandoned Wilkes Station is across the bay. *Thala Dan* can be seen in the bay.

Interestingly, the concrete foundations for the new buildings, require them to be heated while the concrete sets. Otherwise, the concrete just freezes.

Above, across the bay, still stands the American Wilkes Station, which was later handed over to The Australian Antarctic Division. The problem with this station, was that it was built on the ground in a hollow, and was eventually buried by snow, which later turned into ice. It was possible to look down into the hatches of these buildings, and see table, chairs, kitchens, science labs, sleeping quarters, paperwork, cans of food, etc through the clear ice. Wilkes Station buried in ice.

Above two photos of Casey Station were taken whilst in the helicopter. Casey Station is the long tube with adjoining huts. The powerhouse and fuel and emergency radio hut are towards the right, just outside of the picture. The main radio transmitter and receiver huts are further inland from the picture and out of view. The reason for the long corridor, is to link the line of huts together, and allowing the snow to blow under and not build up against the huts. It also enables access to all huts without having to go outside in the environment which is hazardous during winter and blizzards.

The surrounding bay can be clearly seen.

Above picture shows the inside of the long corridor joining the huts.

Above picture shows how the snow is blown underneath the huts to the other side.

Above photo shows the diesel fuel storage, and food for the year stacked up.

A bit about Casey Station location. Casey lies on the Northern side of the Bailey Peninsula overlooking Vincennes Bay on the Budd Coast of Wilkes Land. Casey lies 3,880km due south of Perth, Western Australia. And is built on a rocky outcrop to the ocean. Very rare real-estate as almost all the Antarctic continent is covered in ice to the sea.

After unloading our stores, vehicles, building materials, etc, there is a handing over ceremony. The usual speeches about the work done, and the welcoming of the new expeditioners about to take over for the next 12 months. Then finally the service medallions are handed out to the departing expeditioners. They then leave for the ship, and on the way in the army LARCs, they are traditionally doused with White Flower by the new expeditioners. When the ship turns north and sails off. I again realised that this is home for a long time to come. It's a strange feeling when the ship sails towards the horizon, and this is it.

Above photo shows the handover from the 1980 to the 1981 crew.

Very much like Macquarie, there was enough food supply to last approximately 2 years in case the ship cannot get in during the next summer. Some of the frozen food such as meat, etc was kept in a freezer outdoors next to the buildings. Its main purpose was to keep the food at a constant temperature, and not let it fall too far below zero, as this would shatter the cells of the meat, etc. Home-made beer was also a highlight during the year. As the ingredients were generously donated by Carlton and United Breweries.

As the ice plateau is over 500 metres high behind Casey Station and Law Dome is 1,200 metres high nearby, in the afternoon the air above the plateau and Law Dome cools and becomes heavy. This causes a rush of air, to come rolling down the plateau towards the station. The Katabatic winds can be mild (~15kmph) or quite strong (max recorded gust was 240kmph in March 1992, which is rare event). Most are mild wind gusts late in the afternoons.

Severe cold on a cloudless day. When there are no blizzards and/or no clouds in the sky to keep the warmth in, it is absolutely freezing cold, and easy to get frost bite. The air is bone dry.

Temperature of the air seems to rise during a blizzard. Why I'm not sure. Maybe it's due to the kinetic energy of the wind. Or something else.

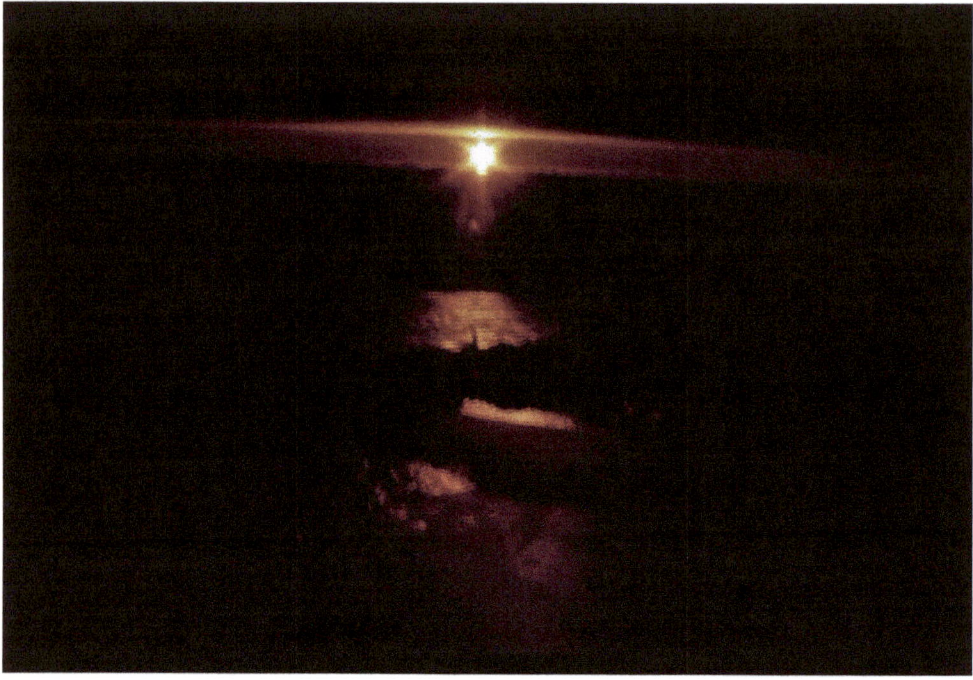

Above below shows the mid-day sun in winter.

Your body clock can go out of kilter if you are not aware of what time it is. It is very important to wake up at the same time each morning. And go to bed at the same time in the evenings. Otherwise, your breakfast becomes lunch and lunch becomes dinner. As Casey is only just outside the Antarctic Circle, we can see the midday sun just come up, down, up again and go down again in a matter of minutes. Two sun rises and sunsets are due to the refraction of the earth's atmosphere on the horizon.

I went outside of the station to observe the Aurora Australis (Southern Lights) one evening. As there was no cloud cover, I was able to take a photo of the aurora's brilliant moving display of colours, like hanging curtains moving in the atmosphere above me. As there was no cloud cover, the temperature was extremely cold. So much so, that there was little time to get your hand out of the gloves to press the button on the SLR camera, and put your hand back in the gloves, without suffering extreme gut-wrenching pain from the hands due to the freezing cold.

Courtesy of blog.com

Behind Casey, and around the bays nearby, there is a line of rocks protruding out from the slowly moving ice towards the coastline, called the moraine. The rocks come from within Antarctica, picked up by the ice movement hundreds or thousands of years ago, and protrude out of the ice near the coastline, as well as near Casey Station. Some of the rocks near Casey also contain gemstones. I found plenty of small pieces of garnet in the rocks. A geologist dream window of what is in the Antarctic rock bed, hundreds, or thousands of km inland from the coast.

CHAPTER 10

DAILY ROUTINES

"VNJ Casey Station" was our radio call sign. Located in the radio hut, were five telex machines connected via radio to other International Antarctic Stations which relayed through Casey VNJ to Sydney OTC radio stations at Bringelly (receiver station) and Doonside (transmitting station). Like that of Macquarie Island communications centre, except a much larger radio and radio relay station. The reliability of Australian communications network enabled several of the other Antarctic Stations as well as our own, to pass their information to Casey, and onto Sydney, and then on to their own countries, as well as our own to Australia.

Other facilities of VNJ were to supply ship to shore communications, and voice over radio for Sydney radio scheds for the expeditioners to Sydney, and for official communications to Head Office and other Antarctic Stations. The workload for the operators was high in demand.

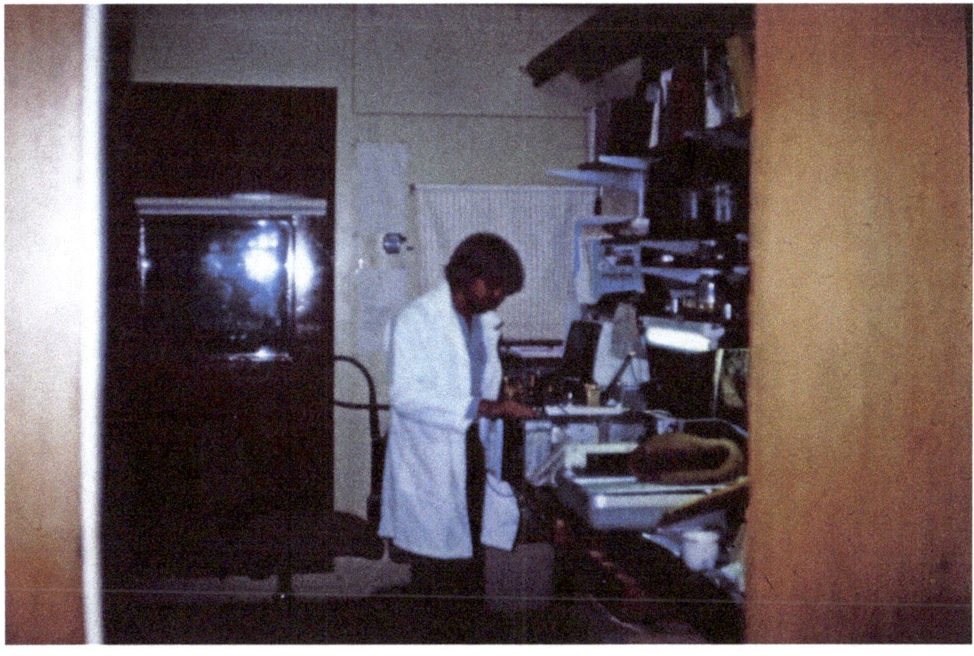

Above in a side room from the radio communications room, was the Radio Technicians workshop. The author in the white coat, of which the station crew thought we technicians were 'boffins. I am pictured repairing an electronic device.

Below are eight radio receivers in the remote receiver site hut, located part of the way towards the plateau, behind Casey Station.

VNJ

Above three photos are the Radio Operators consoles, telex room, and the communications racks to make it all work.

Above is the phone booth, where the expeditioners talked back home on radio schedules at times of the day when radio conditions were good.

A reel-to-reel tape recorder can be seen inside the phone booth. This was used to broadcast 70's music around the station buildings.

Above two photos show the snow track vehicles that the radio technicians needed to get to the remote receiver and transmitter huts and antenna farms in. Herman is in one of the above snow track vehicles, probably contemplating how rough the sastrugi terrain is going to be, while returning to the station. Believe me, it's a rough ride in these conditions.

One afternoon I went to the remote transmitter hut in one of these snow track vehicles. As it happens, one of the tires on the tracks went flat, rendering the snow track disabled, and I was unable to get back to the station. I phoned the station to advise of my situation and of the broken-down snow track vehicle, from the transmitter hut. As there was no one in the radio hut to answer my call, it became a waiting game to get rescued. In the meantime, a blizzard started raging outside. I knew that it was going to be a long night in that transmitter hut, with no place to sleep other than on top of the work bench. My phone call was later answered, and the blizzard was such, that I was advised to stay put and be rescued the next day. Well, there were army rations available (dehydrated food, just add water), and the work bench to sleep on for the night. What a miserable night I had. I couldn't sleep on the floor as it was at freezing temperature, the work bench was at room temperature due to the heat produced by the two 10KW transmitters. The blizzard subsided by the next day. I was lucky in the sense in that these blizzards could last up to 10 days straight.

During the construction of the new building site, rock had to be blasted so that the foundations of the buildings could be built on. One such blast lifted a rock into the air and landed exactly on top of our transmitter cable located between the radio hut and the transmitter hut. The cable was quite a long distance from the blast site, and the odds this happening were very minute. The alarms went off in the radio comms room and Herman's hunch was that the blast may have had something to do with the loss of communications to the transmitter hut. He was right. The weather was clear, and the cable was re-joined.

Note: If the snow track vehicle isn't parked into the wind, this is what happens. A tedious job to dig out the snow from the engine bay and the cabin.

Above is the picture of the two diesel generators, one at a time kept running 24 hours a day in the powerhouse. Without these generators, there would be no electricity, nor hot water going between the buildings to heat the huts. One night, a piston rod went up through the top of the diesel generator, damaging it severely. The diesel mechanics were able to do the repairs and get it back into service. A black and white picture of the damage is towards the end of this book.

The second diesel generator must be started up quickly to maintain hot running water throughout the station. An alarm in the diesel sleeping quarter (donga) alerted the mechanic of engine failure this particular night. Frozen water pipes throughout the station would have be disastrous to the running of the station.

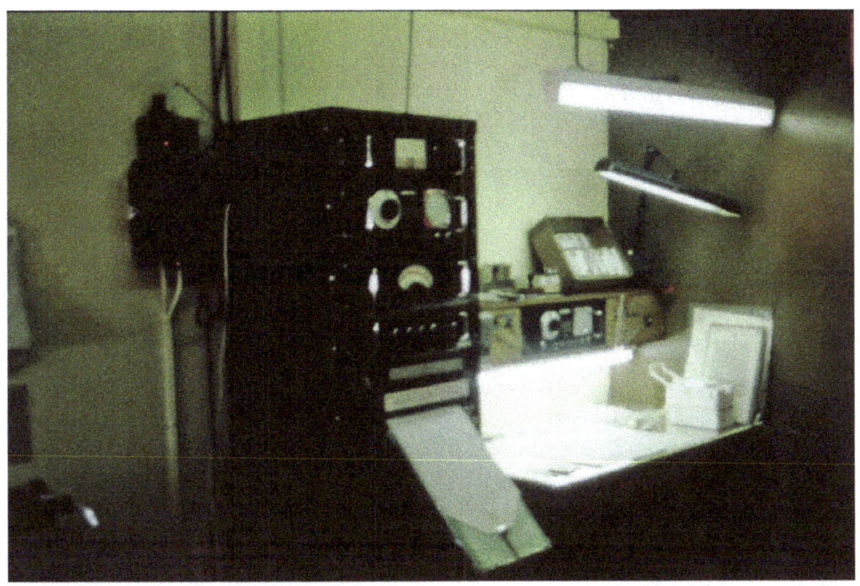

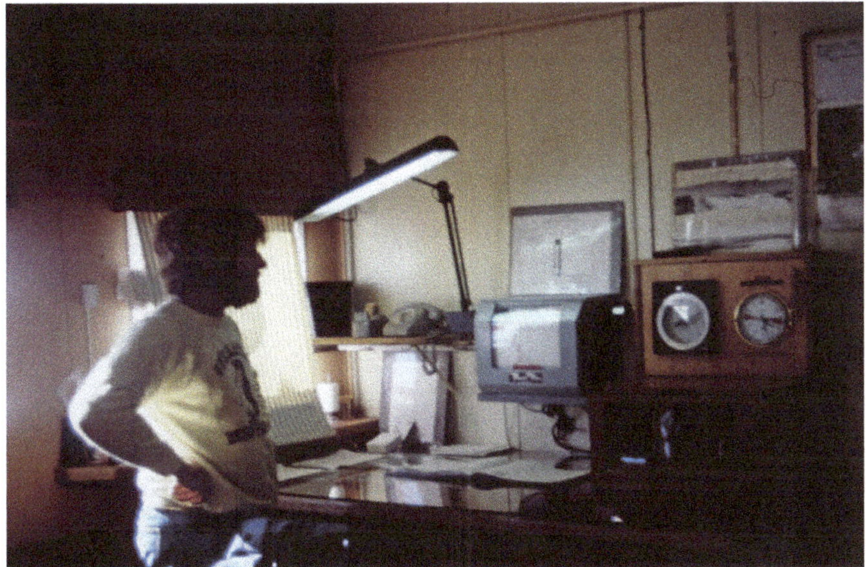

Above is the Meteorological Station at Casey. The red dome near the end of the station corridor, housed the Met Radar which tracked the weather balloon, relaying information back to the weather observers. Beside manual tracking of the balloon, the balloon electronics transmitted weather information to the below instrument recorders. The observers would then relay this information back to Australia via telex, which was used to determine weather forecasts and records for future research on climate change. Very similar to Macquarie Island Meteorological facilities and function.

Above. There was a deep small frozen lake with fresh water below it, just outside of the station. The water would be pumped up into a tank on the back of the tractor and carted regularly to the station storage tank shown below. This water was used for cooking, drinking, showering, washing our clothes, and of course for making our home brew.

Above is the station's water storage tank.

Above two pictures show the field/recreation huts outside of the station. I think the above two photos describe the home comforts provided on outings from the station. Not exactly the Hilton, but they are comfortable enough for a stay over for whatever one is doing in that locale.

Above shows us making coffee in one of the field huts on the other side of the bay from the station. Bruce was one of the radio operators who needed a break from station life also.

Shown above are two of the common vehicles we used to get around in.

Above is the frozen ocean during winter. As viewed from one of the field huts.

The ice at the beginning of winter would congeal and look like pancakes, rubbing together, to eventually form solid sea ice. As shown in the above picture, the ocean is frozen over. During a strong blizzard, the ice could break up, and reform again once the winds subsided.

CHAPTER 11

MAJOR EVENTS

During the summer, one of our diesel mechanics, jack-knifed the large snow track vehicle, which was meant for the traverse during the year, and injured his back. He was sent back to Australia on the next passing ship.

For several months at a time while the diesel mechanics and scientists (Glaciologist, engineer, and surveyor) were out on traverse, the rest of us were stationed at Casey Station, maintaining communications, weather reports and scientific collection of data. Another team brought down for the following summer, would be at Cape Folger drilling an ice core to the bottom of the ice sheet, to the land mass below.

I was asked would I like to go on traverse for 3 weeks. My job, using RADAR was to measure the ice depth to the underlying rock bead. Record it on film as we travelled inland high up on the plateau. And develop the film while bouncing along in the caravan on skis, drawn by a D5 Caterpillar grader.

The D5 Caterpillar would have its front blade down attempting to make a smooth road ahead, as the sastrugi would be severe for travel without the way made smooth.

The other expeditioner in the instrument van with me, was constantly looking into a navigation type radar screen, searching for the next cane planted into the ice during a previous traverse. Once the cane is found (a white dot on the radar screen), the train stops and a GPS measurement is taken to determine the location of the cane, which determines how much the ice has travelled towards the coast or elsewhere since the last traverse. The height of the cane is measured to determine how much snow has fallen in this location. When a new route is required, the surveyor or other professional does the navigation. The cane line is also useful in returning to the station. Just follow the radar dots. The D5 Caterpillar train travels at about 5km per hour in my year on the ice. If the weather was calm, I would walk along side of the train for kilometres just to keep fit, and, I liked space whereas the caravans tended to be claustrophobic to me back then.

Above is a picture of the canes which are inserted into the ice to be measured by another traverse in later years. Or to replace those which have been buried by snow.

Above shows us traversing through blizzards which could last for 10 days or more, especially during the winter months. Also above is a picture of the food storage located on the rear of the instrument van.

Above two pictures are of the D5 Caterpillar leading the way with the caravan in tow. Note the flat, white, desolate environment that we lived in during the traverses. To focus one's eyes on the ice is very difficult, resulting on little visual or mental stimulation. About 3 days into the traverse, I heard similar comments that one feels a little mentally ill due to this for one day. I felt the same way.

Picture above shows the sastrugi, making travel rough. Sastrugi is the surface of the ice roughened by the winds over time. In the distance are the receiver station and antennas.

Taken in winter with the late sun lighting up the northern horizon in the above picture. And close to getting back to the coastline after our 3 weeks traversing the icy continent. From left to right of the picture, diesel fuel sled, then the diesel engine for power of lighting, heating, and electronics, and for heating of the D5 Caterpillar engine sump when the train stops overnight, and showers and cooking. Then the third van from the left is the instrument van with sleeping quarters, ice depth measurement equipment, radar, and communications. This instrument van had the food supply on its rear end. Then in the front is the D5 Caterpillar.

There was a special case in the past, on one of the Australian Antarctic Stations, of ingenuity and great skill required, where the heater in the D5 engine sump failed and the engine cracked in half from the extreme cold. The diesel mechanic welded the engine together and drove it back to their station. The D5 Caterpillar is now in a Caterpillar Museum in the USA, on display.

A traverse consists of three trains. In case of one not able to return to the station for whatever reason like D5 Caterpillar engine failure, fallen in a crevasse (as did happen outside of Casey Station in my year), etc. the other two trains can return to the station with safety due to redundancy.

Pictured above is 'Blue' operating the radar, locating the cane line of which we must follow.

Above two pictures are the scientific measurements, Gravity measurement and GPS readings, in the box with the antenna outside for our cane location, etc.

Below 5 photos show as well as the surface entrance to a large research tent now buried under the ice from years ago, the tunnel going down into it. The hole to it is kept clear by placing a hatch over it and raised by visitors regularly to clear the build-up of snow. The buried tent still houses a petrol generator, table, and various left-over scientific items.

Above picture, at the entrance to this research tent just described, is a sign. Also note the large ice crystals on the right that have grown over time in the tunnel to the tent.

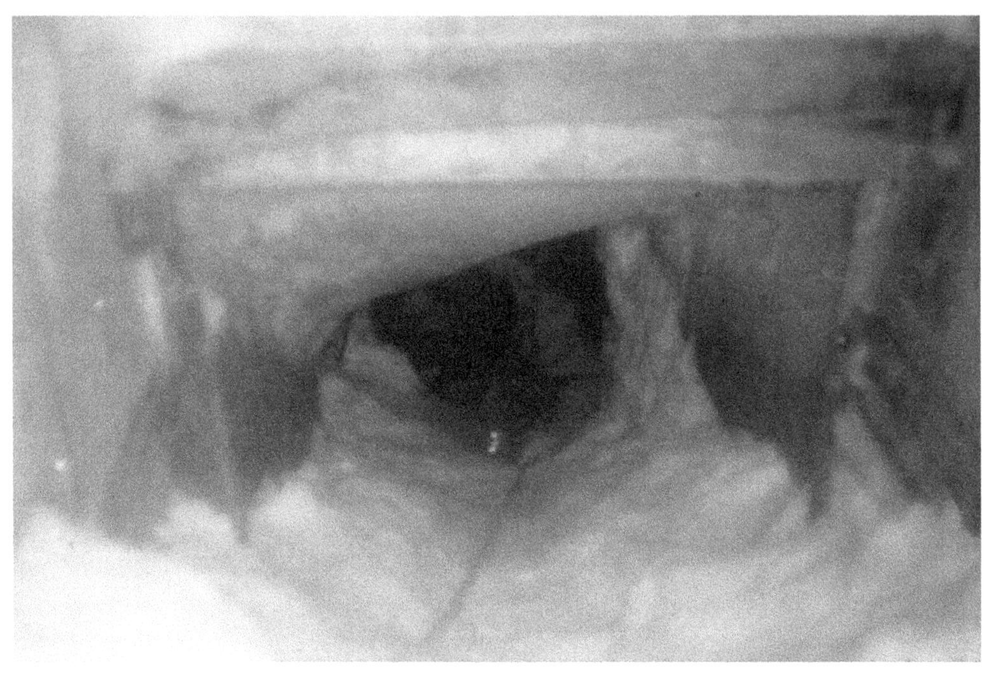

Above is the buried tent still accessible, though slowly caving in by the ice surrounding it.

Above is a plane found almost buried in the ice, which never made it back from where it came from.

A sunset as we approached the coastline, returning to Casey Station in the traverse train.

At the start of the following summer, ice drilling project nearby Casey Station at Cape Folger successfully retrieved some 300m deep core from the summit of Cape Folger through to the underlying bedrock. This involved a new computer-controlled drill and control system. A special circular ice melt head drill was used. The ice cores would give up clues to what the earth's atmosphere was like hundreds and thousands of years ago. Air from the past would be trapped in the snow and eventually into the ice due to the pressure of the above ice, which would build up over the centuries. To look at this ancient ice, one couldn't see any air bubbles in the ice core. The pressure under the ice is so great, that the air is forced into the lattice of the ice. It just looked like clear ice, until one places a small sample into our drinks while watching a movie. And it was impossible to hear the movie, due to the small explosions of air molecules from this ice when it thawed out in our drinks.

Above is the ice core drill rig at Cape Folger. 1981. Not far from Casey Station.

Above is the author within the ice core storage facility at Cape Folger.

In later years, ice drilling at Law Dome summit drilling went down to 1200 metres, enabling the scientists back in Australia to study the ice cores.

During the year, one of our expeditioners fell ill. The medical doctors in Melbourne assisted with our doctor via a radio linkup, to cut him open and find out what the problem was. During the operation, the radio link to Sydney OTC Bringelly Receiving Station failed, and the patient was still on the operating table. As Herman had an amateur radio licence, he called several amateur radio enthusiasts for help in contacting OTC Paddington (Sydney) to reconnect to our station. Herman was able to contact an amateur Station in NSW to telephone Paddington OTC for us and hence the doctors were communicating again. As I have been at this receiving station during my training years, I knew what happened there with the receiver. The operation revealed nothing and therefore the patient was sewn up. He was later evacuated to Australia by aircraft via McMurdo Sound.

One of my front tooth fillings fell out. As the doctor had some training in dentistry before leaving for Casey, he attempted to replace my filling. The filing lasted a couple of days only, before falling out. I decided just to leave it until I returned home.

During the winter, the blizzards would last 10 days on, and 10 days off, constantly. Not so much in the summer months, though blizzards were still unpredictable.

The howling winds are deafening, and impossible to walk anywhere in. Visibility is zero. One could not see one's hands in a blizzard. During the 1979 expedition to Casey, one of the expeditioners overstaying in a remote field/recreational hut, decided to walk to the nearby toilet outside. With no rope between the huts, he probably thought that he could walk directly to the hut. During the short walk, he was buffeted by the high winds and missed the toilet location as visibility also was down to zero. He was found frozen the next morning on the ice nearby. The year prior to us, 1980, saw his coffin loaded onto the ship that summer for return to Australia.

Everywhere one looks, there are severe life-threatening hazards in Antarctica.

- Crevasses are prolific around the coastline, and so around Casey Station. They can be open, or covered in a snow bridge, being hard to see until one walked on it, or a snow vehicle attempts to ride over it. This happened outside of Casey Station in our year, where one of the D5 Caterpillars, decided to take a short cut around the crevasses, and ended up in one of them, with the D5 Caterpillar rear sticking out. The diesel mechanics came to the rescue and pulled the D5 out. Many of these crevasses are recorded onto a map near the station, so this should not have happened.

- Scientists were dropped on to a glacial flow from a helicopter, to do scientific research and data collecting. They radioed back to the station for the helicopter to return to pick them up. The scientists used a flare to indicate their location on the ice shelf. As the wind was blowing, the flare smoke was also blowing sideways. To the helicopter pilot, this gave the appearance that he was flying higher than what he was. When flying over ice, one's eyes cannot focus on the ice as it is all white and its distance away is unknown at the time. So, the pilot came down towards the ice and misjudged the height of it and slammed into the ice shelf. And at the same time as realising his mistake, he pulled up. One helicopter skis broke off and the only alternative was to return to the station as it was impossible to land there without skis. He radioed back to the station, stating what the dilemma of landing with no skis was, and the helicopter blades spinning on landing would be hazardous once the blades hit the ground in the obvious likelihood of the helicopter falling over. Several tradesmen rigged up a row of 44-gallon drums for the helicopter to land on. The helicopter arrived and gently landed on the drums. The tradesmen went forward to the landed helicopter with its blades spinning and held it on both sides until the blades stopped. A crane was brought over, and the helicopter was attached to it, holding it up so that it wouldn't fall over. A second helicopter went out and picked up the scientists stranded on the glacier later that day. The bravery of the expeditioners sent to these stations is amazing. I think once you are down there, survival instincts of self and for others kick in.

Above. One helicopter with missing skis, held up by a crane. It was later lifted onto the barge and sent back to Australia for repairs.

On one of my stayovers in a field hut on the other side of the bay from Casey, we three decided to stay for the night. After melting some ice for cooking dinner, and dining Antarctic field style, we turned in for the night. Heating of the hut was done with a kerosene heater in the centre of the hut. Airflow into the hut was done via the hatch kept open with a matchbox, and the door ventilation hole opened. During the night, I woke up with stinging eyes and difficulty breathing. Carbon Monoxide (CO) build up I thought, though I couldn't understand why. I examined the hatch, and the matchbox was moved sideways, closing the hatch. I examined the door ventilator, and it was also closed. I immediately opened both vents and woke the other two expeditioners. One of them admitted that he was getting cold and therefore closed the hatch and door ventilator. Other expeditioners in past years have died from this very CO poisoning whilst in their accommodation.

On a cloudless freezing cold day out on the ice, I didn't realise that I was getting frost bite on my face cheeks. One of the expeditioners came over and noticed the white frozen skin on my face, removed his hand from the glove and warmed up my face until it thawed out. This must have been a painful exercise for him, as once the hand is outside the glove for any more than a few seconds or so, the hand becomes excruciating painful from the extreme cold. I was very grateful.

I decided to build an igloo whilst staying over at the ice drilling platform at Cape Folger, and to see how the very early expeditioners lived and survived whilst traversing the continent with huskies. I pulled out two sleeping bags and slept in both, one inside the other which is what we do in extreme cold weather. Two problems arose. One, snow drift is so fine, it is like dry talcum powder and will fill any cavity quickly, including vehicles. The second was that I like space, including when I sleep in a sleeping bag. The fine snow drift partially filled my igloo, and when I woke my left arm was outside of the sleeping bag. My arm was cold as meat in a fridge, and there was no feeling or movement from it. Knowing from my survival training for hypothermia, I put the arm into the sleeping bag next to my body so it could thaw out slowly. Which it did, thereby saving my left arm.

At the end of winter and during the spring, algae from the coastal ocean floor can rise and attach itself to the bottom of the sea ice near the station and nearby islands. Also a seal could leave a slight brown mark on the sea ice. In this case I wasn't sure what caused this sea ice brown stain which proved to be very soft to walk on. It was on a sunny spring day, wearing only sneakers, jeans, and long sleeve shirt (as it was relatively warm, about -2 degrees Celsius with no wind (as we were acclimatised to the cold well and truly by then), I decided to catch up with the other expeditioners who left earlier to go to one of the very nearby islands, that had a penguin rookery on it. I was walking quickly to catch up, and not realising what the light brown stain was on the sea ice, attempted to walk across it. Before I knew it, I was swimming the ocean, with my legs kicking so fast, that I slid up onto the sea ice like a penguin. The walk back to the station was uncomfortable, like severe skin irritations from the coldness of the sea water -2 degrees Celsius. I stood under a lukewarm shower when I reached the station ablutions, and my skin was red raw in colour, and itchy. Had I been wearing the heavy Antarctic clothing; I would have gone to the bottom of the bay.

As it was enticing to climb an iceberg in the winter months near the ice cliffs where Casey stood, I did so. Understanding that most of the berg was underwater, and solid so I thought. I thought it would be safe to climb to the top and back to shore again. On reaching part of the way to its top, I put the ice axe into the berg, noting that it was mostly hardened snow. Hastily I climbed down thinking that this is not good. The next day, we were near this same position up on the ice cliff above this iceberg, when suddenly it broke in half and began to roll outwards in the ocean, breaking up the sea ice as it went.

This same day of observing the iceberg break in two and rolling in the ocean and breaking up the sea's ice as it went, we were chatting away, sitting on the ice where we thought was plenty of distance between us and the ice cliff face. NO! Suddenly there was a loud shot gun blast sound between us and the cliff face, caused by a fine crack in the ice sheet just in front of us, and between us and the snow track vehicle that we had to get back to the station in. The snow vehicle also had our radio and survival equipment in it. There was no discussion about what to do. It was unanimous to get out of there as quickly as possible. So, we headed back to the station after all that. We had enough adventures for the past two days.

Above shows the snow track vehicle and us. Between us and the vehicle, a fine crack appeared in the ice, sounding like a shot gun blast.

Summer scientists and crew flew into Casey on an American Hercules C130 plane. The airstrip was graded by the diesel mechanics with their D5 Caterpillars. The American plane loaded the Casey personnel and cargo, and readied to fly off, back to the American McMurdo station. The plane was not able to stay long, nor could the propellers be stopped due to the cold as the engines would freeze up. From hearsay of one of our expeditioners, our crew at the plane site felt awkward in greeting the new summer crew at first. I guess it was due to our long isolation, nine months of history, and therefore having to adjust to new members to the expedition.

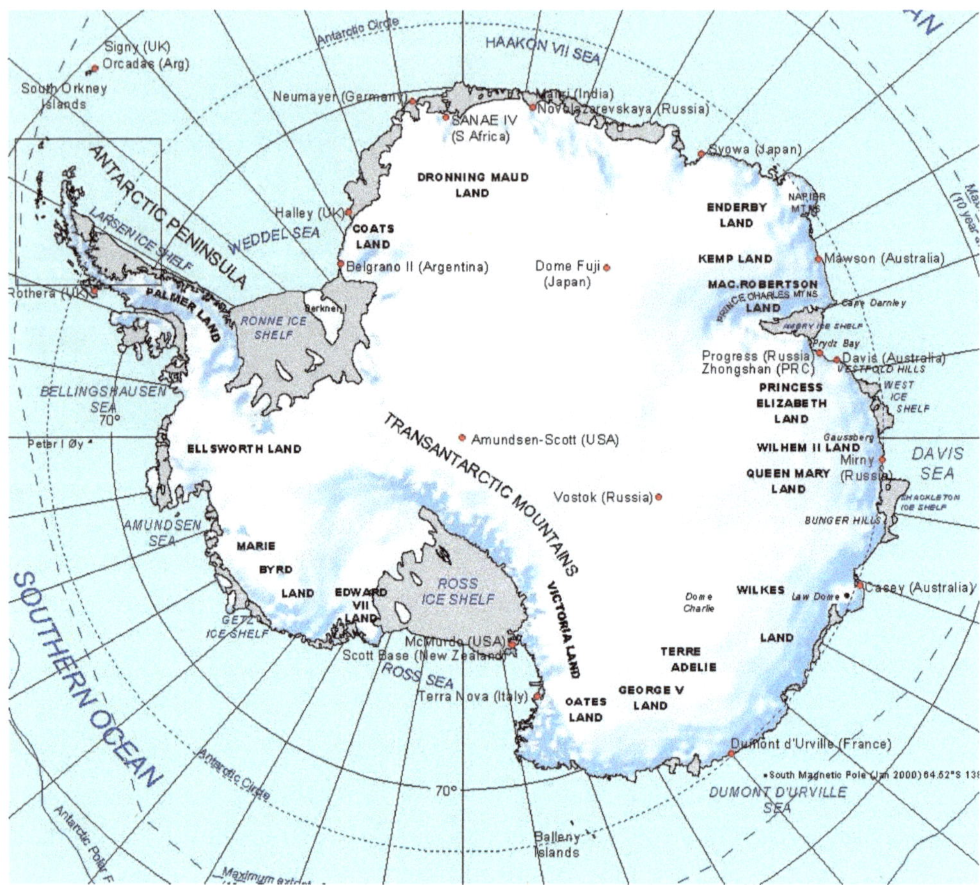

Courtesy: blogspot.com

It was up to me to drive two scientists around the top of the bay near Casey Station, to the ice cliffs, where they wanted to do some research on the sea ice from there. I parked the snow track vehicle at the top of the cliff face, and we climbed down to the sea ice and walked about 100 metres or so towards the ocean. While the scientists were doing their measurements and data collection from the sea ice, I noticed the Southern horizon and the Moraine Line disappear (The Moraine Line is a line of rocks protruding from the plateau ice). I told the scientists that it was urgent to leave and get back to the station immediately as there was a blizzard coming in quickly. Knowing that the blizzard was going to hit us before we reached the ice cliffs, I put the men in a straight line pointing towards the snow track vehicle. The blizzard did hit us before we reached the cliff, but because we were in a straight line and the expeditioner in front kept checking his rear to keep the line straight as possible, we quite accurately reached the ice cliff and to the vehicle directly at the top, Visibility was very low at this stage. I could not see through the blizzard while driving back to the station, so my survival instincts went into high gear. If I drove too low around the bay, we would have gone over the ice cliff into the ocean. If I drove too high around the bay curvature, I would have hit the Moraine Line and damaged the tracks of the snow track vehicle, gotten stuck in the rocks, or disappeared onto the plateau in the blizzard. I managed to keep the same angle of the vehicle going around the bay until I sensed that soon I would reach the cane line going down the station. I had poor visibility and knew that if we didn't get back to the station, we might not survive the blizzard. None of the scientists knew how much trouble we were in, nor have I ever let on until now to anyone associated with the year. I sensed that there was soon to be a cane sticking up to show us the way down to the station, and within minutes, I could just see it to the right of me. A sharp turn to the right, then the next cane came out of the blizzard, and thereby I straightened up and headed for the station, following the cane line. My survival instincts saved us that day.

Above and below are the ice cliffs and the bay that I was just describing.

Here I am near the ice cliff described above. I was getting some much needed sunshine on my back while the air temperature was mild and with no wind. A blizzard later in the day was going to give us grief, and a problem of getting back to the station safely.

CHAPTER 12

SOCIAL INTERACTIONS

Casey Station entertainment: Canned beer was supplied and rationed weekly. It was also used as currency for horse race events screened from my computer to the television. I programmed the horse race on my System 80 Dick Smith computer which became available on the market before I left for Casey. My programming was written in Basic. I made a terrible error in the odds calculation for 1st, 2nd and 3rd place, and as being the 'bank', I lost all my beer rations on the first night. Before the computerised race began, I would sound the "Assembly of the Buglers" on my trumpet, and then the horse race would begin.

Herman wrote in machine code on my computer to decode telex messages from a new but faulty message storage machine, and then the computer would translate it to the monitor screen in text. It was exciting in these days, as personal computers had only just become available, and we could see the potential for these machines.

Reel to reel movies twice a week was another highlight for us. We were also given VHS tapes and watched movies on the television screen in the recreational hut.

The recreational hut with the bar, was often a meeting place after work. There we could relax and wind down after a long day working. Or on the Sunday, the day off, we would use the library there or play on the billiard table. The canned beer was kept there in our own personal shelf, and we would leave it outside the door for a few minutes to chill it before drinking it.

Very popular volleyball would be played when the weather allowed it, which certainly was not the case during the winter season. Indoors, would see the bowls tournament.

A disco on the stations roof top and a BBQ below was enjoyed by many expeditioners on this day. The two speaker boxes in the picture were both put together by me from a design in a very old radio handbook found in the radio workshop. The radio operators had plenty of the latest 70's music, loaded onto a reel-to-reel tape deck from the radio hut, and we connected it to the roof top speakers. A previous radio technician built a small radio station KOLD (for 1981 it was renamed KLOD), which transmitted our own programs from the reel-to-reel tape recorder over radio and the telephone lines between the huts, located from the rear of the radio operations room. Down below was the BBQ. It was cold enough for our fingers to freeze to the plates.

RADIO
VNJ

Above is the Recreation Room with its own bar.

Board skiing down slopes near the station is a favourite past time. Also, there were a couple of skidoos on the station for fun, riding up and down the slopes.

Plenty of books to read from the station's library.

As there were no hair stylists on the station, we had to do it ourselves. I saw how the other expeditioners cut each other's hair. Their hair styles didn't impress me, so I let mine just grow long. I did attempt to cut Herman's hair once, but it came out rather odd and short.

Our Chef, Glen was exceptional in preparing for special occasions, such as for birthdays, Mid-Winter Celebrations, October Fest, etc, and of course Christmas. Dressed here in his refinery.

The kitchen was large and easy to use. All expeditioners, like on Macquarie and the other Australian Antarctic Stations, took turns to cook on a Sunday. During the week, the same expeditioner would help in the kitchen during the day, prepare breakfast and do other slushy duties. Another expeditioner would stay up every night for a week, to do 'fire watch' duties. A fire here or on any station would be catastrophic, as the air in Antarctica is bone dry.

There were about 28 to cook for, when there were no traverses out in the field. About 19 of us that were permanently on the station otherwise, about 9 expeditioners would spend 3 months at a time on a traverse, inland to do scientific research on the ice.

Above is Glen and his kitchen. A very important and much appreciated position on the station.

Above is the Casey Station kitchen and the mess on the other side of the servery. Our diesel mechanic, Lennie's turn to cook for the team.

Mid-Winter's celebration is celebrated on the shortest day of the year, in June. A traditional mid-winter's swim in the ocean was supported by most of us. The ocean temperature at the shore is about -5 degrees Celsius. So, it's a very quick in and out, before hypothermia sets in. My swim at Macquarie Island was a balmy +5 degrees Celsius.

The mid-winter's celebration is a formal affair, dressed in our ANARE supplied suits and tie. The last time we dressed up like this, was our departure from Melbourne on the ice breaker *Thala Dan*.

Above picture shows the post celebratory midwinter dinner drinks in the recreation hut. Photos on the wall are of previous expeditioners groups taken at mid-winter of their year.

Above mid-winter's celebrations come with the customary 'Cinderella' play, and other plays designed by clever and entertaining script writers on the station.

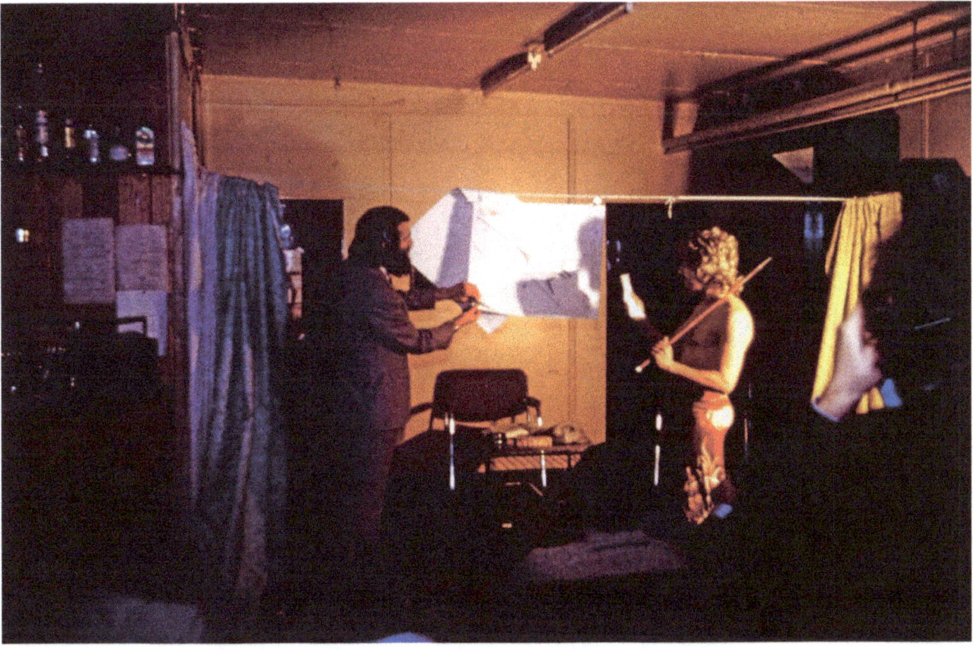

I couldn't see myself as one of the Cinderella sisters. But of course I joined in as a 'Weather Girl', with Herman having written the script and performed with me above as well.

Pictured above is the Mid-Winter's group photo – Casey 1981. This photo was sent back to Australia via radio facsimile, to head office, to then be passed onto our friends and families.

Above, it was our turn to greet the newcomers, the '82ers, after we endured as an expeditionary force for 12 months at Casey. A welcoming with our huge smoke ring from the explosion of the old diesel stored in drums near the foreshore.

Heading home aboard the *Thala Dan*. Let's call into Macquarie Island on the way home. The author for a short period at the helm of *Thala Dan*.

It was a joy to call into Macquarie Island (summer of 1982) after living and leaving there 3 years ago. To see the work I'd done there and everything radio-wise was still in good condition, and our year group photo on the mess wall with all the other previous years. I reminisced on what transpired there in 1978/79 and remembered what a tough 15 months it was for me.

Macquarie Island, 'The Jewel of the South Pacific'. The Casey expeditioners were pleased to see greenery and an abundance of wildlife at Macquarie.

Pictured above and below, is the top of North Heads looking down at the Island's station, and the *Thala Dan* in the distance.

Above we are returning to the *Thala Dan* via the Army LARCS, bound for home.

Below, now looking forward to our destination. Home, Australia, in the distance.

35 years later, a Casey Station expeditioner 7th reunion was held in Darwin, 2016. A heartfelt get together to remember the times at Casey, and retell the stories about Casey, 1981.

Above are the Casey '81 expeditioners that could make it to Darwin for the reunion.

Above and below, relaxing in Darwin before and after our formal midwinter's dinner. With old mates once again.

Above: Some of the wives of the 81' Casey expeditioners.

His Excellency General the Honourable Sir Peter Cosgrove AK MC (Retd)
Governor-General of the Commonwealth of Australia

Casey Expeditioners – 35 Year Renunion

It takes a special type of person to live and work in the extreme conditions of the Antarctic.

But the very fact that after some 35 years so many Casey Expeditioners have made another great expedition—this time to the top end—to remember and celebrate their time together is testament to the depth of the experience and the bonds that were forged.

I am sure each and every one of you are proud of the contribution you made, whether it was ice drilling, rebuilding the stations or making home brew! You worked as a team, as a community, and you will always be part of Australia's role in this important continent.

And of course, let's not forget your families and loved ones who missed you and kept things ticking along when you were away, and we also remember your colleagues who are no longer with us.

Have a great night.

GOVERNMENT HOUSE CANBERRA ACT 2600 AUSTRALIA
TELEPHONE +61(2) 6283 3533 FACSIMILE +61(2) 6281 3760
WWW.GG.GOV.AU

A letter above, to each of us, from our Governor General of Australia, regarding our 35th year reunion in 2016.

The recent 8th Casey Station Reunion in 2021, was held in Brisbane. It was voted whilst we were all in Darwin for the 35th reunion, that Brisbane is the place to celebrate our 40 year reunion. As I am the only one living in Brisbane, it became my job to prepare for our reunion near the shortest day of the year being in June. The formal midwinters dinner was held at a classy function venue in the city on the Saturday.

Above shows the expeditioners that were able to make the reunion in Brisbane during the covid 19 pandemic. Several states in the country were in 'lock down', preventing several members from attending. We were able to have a 'zoom video' meeting via the internet in my home on the following day with them.

Above is the author with my then partner, Michiko.

Above is Michiko organising the catering in my kitchen. Below is the gathering of expeditioners in the patio outside. It was of middle winter, though the evening was mild and comfotrable with the infra-red heaters on. Reminiscing once again went on long into the night.

Above 'zoom video' meetup with some of the expeditioners who couldn't make it to the Brisbane reunion.

CHAPTER 13

CASEY STATION WILDLIFE

Above is a Skua which like on Macquarie, cleans up carcases in penguin rookeries and dead seals during the summer and preventing diseases from forming throughout the rookeries. Wildlife at Casey disappears during the winter.

Above is an Adelie penguin rookery on one of the islands nearby to the station.

Above is a male Adelie penguin waiting for his partner after making a stone nest.

Above is a pair of Adelie penguins during their courtship. They mate for life.

Above is a male Adelie with two large chicks to look after.

Above is a King penguin during the summer of 1982 at Macquarie Island, on the way back from Casey.

Above are two Emperor penguins on an ice flow during the summer near Casey Station, 1981.

Above is an elephant seal on an iceberg.

Above is the size that the moss will grow to, and the different colours. Something of interest, Tetanus is known to survive here in the rookeries.

CHAPTER 14

CASEY STATION "BLACK & WHITE"

My Aunty Ethyl and close cousin Deb seeing me off on the *Thala Dan* to Casey Station. Location Port of Melbourne.

Above is the author about to board the *Thala Dan* for an adventure unknown at Casey Station, Antarctica.

Below is the sharp defining line of sea ice surrounding Antarctica during the summer. A helicopter is needed to show the ship captain a safe passage through the ice, to Casey station.

The *Thala Dan* from the helicopter located near Casey Station.

Above was a welcoming 'blast' for the 1981 expeditioners when we entered the bay.

Above is the Vanderford Glacier, to the left of the station facing north. It is about 5 km wide jutting out into the ocean

Above is Casey Station from the helicopter, 1981

243

Above is the Casey Station corridor joining all the huts together.

Above is part of the station with the Meteorology balloon launching shed at the far left.

Above is the construction of the new Casey Station. Nearby is the old Casey Station. Completion of new station was in 1988.

Above is the radio team with the two radio snow track vehicles, and the VNJ Radio Hut behind. Three radio operators, Bruce, Mick, and Lindsay on the left. Radio techs Herman and myself on the right of the picture.

Above is what happens when one doesn't park the vehicle into the wind of a blizzard.

Above two photos show our new to the market, a Dick Smith System 80 personal computer. I am programming it for a horse race, with eight horses racing across the screen. It was used as entertainment in the recreation hut. Random odds were calculated for each horse. Herman later programmed the computer to read telex messages and then bring it up on the screen as text. And to read telex signals required to repair a telex device on the station.

The two above photos are of the technician's workshop, with the author and two of our three radio operators, Lindsay, and Mick.

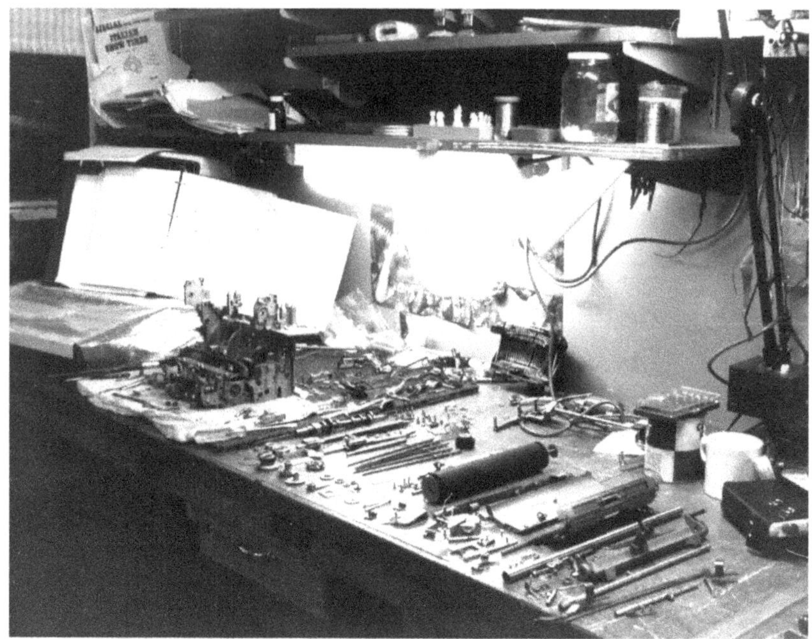

Above shows my attempt to repair and do maintenance on one of our Teleprinter Machines for the first time. Just follow the manual. Assembling it was not easy, but I managed to get it back together again, working.

Above picture show how our Summer water supply is carted back from a melt lake near the new building site.

Above is Herman in the Emergency Radio Hut, calling for assistance to get the Overseas Telecommunications Commission (Aust) Receiving Station in Sydney (Bringelly) to come back online during a crucial time while our doctor was operating on one of our expeditioners, and consulting with the medical doctors in Australia at the same time. The OTC radio link was eventually re-established with help from a NSW radio amateur enthusiast. The patient survived.

Above picture show the Emergency Radio Hut.

Above show the bay in front of the station, sea ice having interest for scientists and station personnel.

Above two photos show several scientists and support crew drilling into the sea ice for some research data they needed.

Below four photos depicts one of several celebrations. This one was for The October Fest.

Above is Lyndsay our radio operator having a good time, including all the Casey crew.

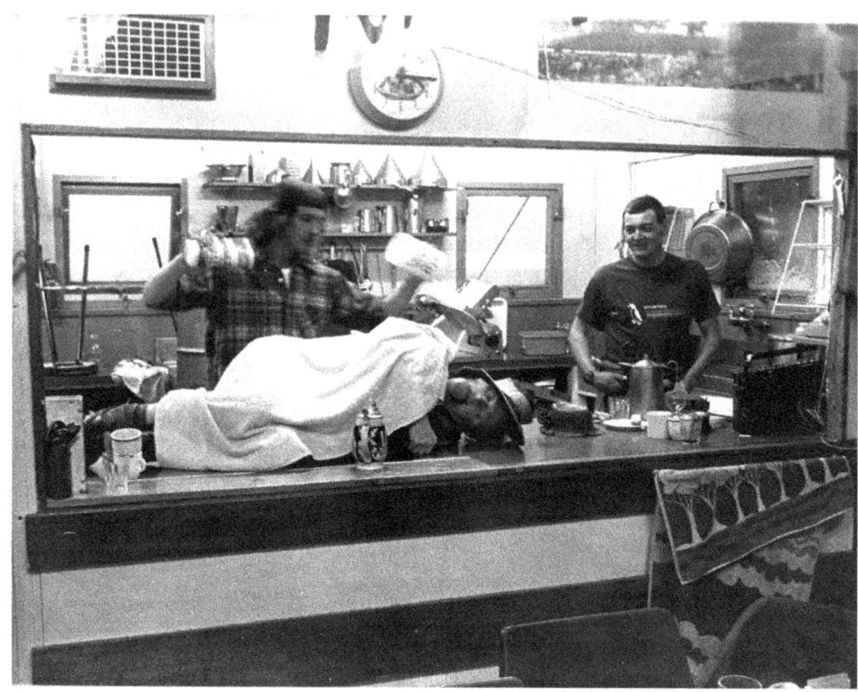

Above are some antics in the kitchen.

Above picture show these expeditioners coming for lunch as "surfies". Though the surf at Casey was a little flat.

Above is our Christmas Celebrations.

Above, handing out our Christmas presents on Christmas day.

Above is Christmas lunch.

Above picture as seen by the Diesel OIC, thought this was very funny and roared with laughter when I posted it up on the mess notice board. It's impossible for this small snow track vehicle that belongs to the radio section, to pull a sledge full of diesel fuel.

Above is one of the several field huts around the bay near Casey Station.

Above picture show the traverse team about to leave Casey and go into the remote parts of the continent and to do scientific measurements of the ice.

Above two photos show two of the three traverse trains out on traverse somewhere far inland.

Above is the diesel fuel for the traverse, carried behind one of the caravans.

Above is somewhere far from Casey, inland, with the caravan on the right, with light snow drift.

Above is an expeditioner navigating using radar, following the white dots on the screen which indicates the cane line of which we were following.

Above, the author recording the ice thickness above the rock bed far below on film as we travelled.

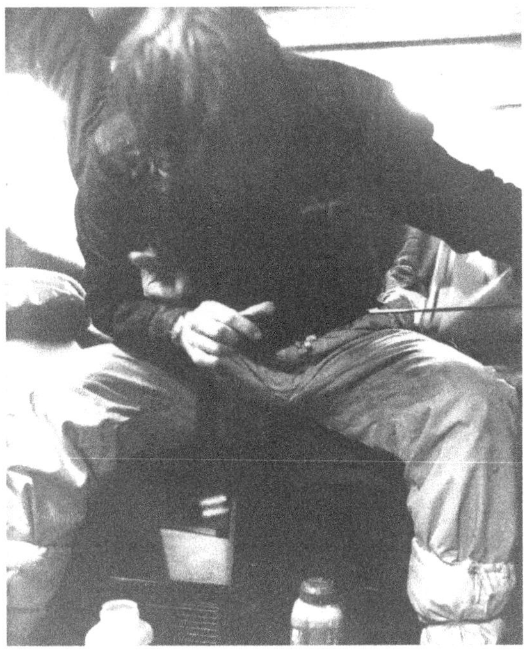

Above, above the author is developing the film whilst travelling in the instrument van.

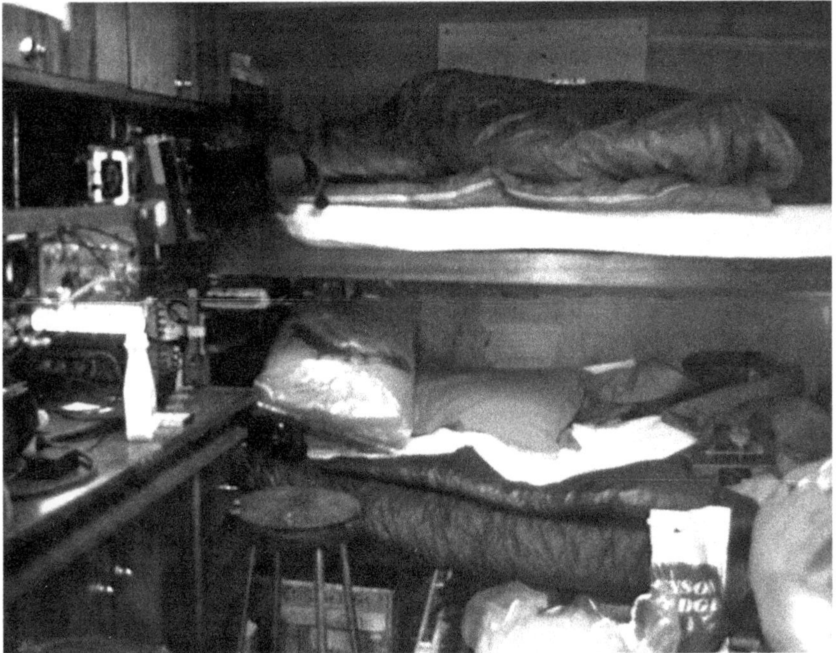

Above is the inside of this instrument van, the radar on the left, and the sleeping bunks on board

Above is the author working outside on the ice radar antennae, which are used to measure the ice thickness, and of the rock bed surface terrain. A radio pulse is transmitted down into the ice. As the ice is transparent to these radio signals, the radio signal bounces off the rock bed below, and is received by the instrument van receiver. Using the time difference, and the signal takes to travel down to the rock bed and come up, the distance can easily be calculated.

Above, the author is putting up the radio antenna, for communications back to Casey Station. We were in the middle of a blizzard at the time. We were about 1.4km high above the rock bed, camped on the ice.

Above, I am making coffee by melting pure snow.

Below four pictures describe the ice drilling project at Cape Folger, at nearby Casey station. Drilling 300 metre depth to the rock bed and sending the ice cores back to the glaciology lab in Australia for analysis, as discussed previously. The fourth picture below is of the drill itself looking down from above in the cone tower.

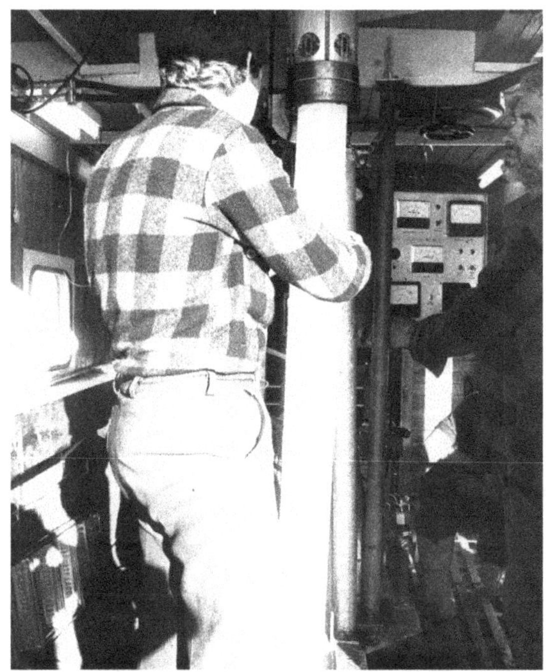

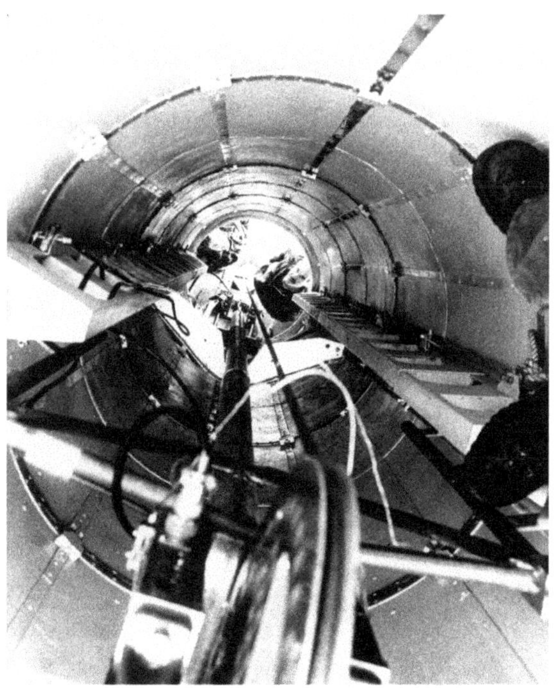

Once the ice drill approaches the rock bed, the temperature of the ice increases due to the friction of the moving ice on the rock bed below. It then becomes 'slushy'. A mixture of ice and water.

Above is the Moraine Line at the back of Casey. These rocks are picked up by the ice flow from the inner continent and dropped off at the coastline. A geologist dream to study the inner Antarctic continent rocks from here. Pictured here is the Station OIC, Joe.

Above is one of our diesel mechanics doing repairs to the diesel generator which failed during the year.

Above are Adelie penguins, pushing the front penguins into the sea, to see if there are any predators in the water, before diving in themselves.

Above is an Adelie penguin feeding its chick.

Above is an Adelie penguin rookery on a nearby island.

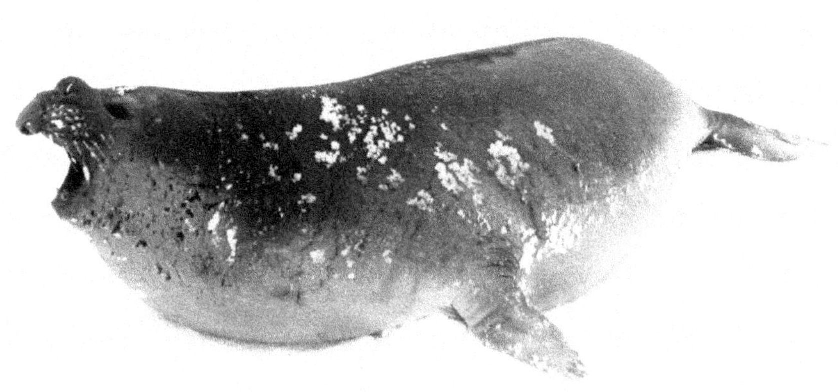

Above two photos show seals of various types which frequent Casey during the summer. Such as Weddell seals, elephant seals, etc.

Above I managed to capture a picture of a Wandering Albatross flying past the *Thala Dan* on our way to Casey Station.

Above is an Emperor penguin near one of the station's islands.

Above is one of several Huskies that were removed from Casey Station in 1980, a year before our arrival. All introduced species were to be removed from Antarctica except humans, in 1991. (Antarctic Treaty declaration).

Above three pictures, a cairn left by Americans with an American flag, somewhere down the coast from Casey.

Above is a sobering picture of two lives lost at Wilkes Station across the bay from Casey Station. More lives were lost in later years at Casey Station.

Pictures of my Antarctic service medals of Macquarie and Casey Station, given to me at the changeover of the expeditioner's year ceremony on both Stations.

Macquarie Island 1978   Casey 1981

Bibliography

MAAS. Description of the adventures of David Lewis.

References:

1. Royal Australian Navy, Navy News, Vol. 22, No. 1, 26 January 1979.

2. HMAS *Hobart*, Report of Proceedings, January 1979.

The rescue of Mr Roger Barker is mentioned in Tim Bowden, 'The Silence Calling, Australians in Antarctica 1947-97', Allen & Unwin, St Leonards, NSW, 1997, pp. 351-352

Acknowledgement

A special thanks to DR. Andrew Bode and to DR. Margaret Demarco-Messinbird (Margie). Without Andrew's and Margie's suggestions and encouragement that I should record my experiences, and with guidance, deletions and inclusions to my text and photos, this book would not have been written.

A thank you to Herman Westerhof (Casey Radio OIC) for ensuring that the Casey content was historically correct to the best our knowledge.

To the Macquarie 1978/79, and Casey 1981 expeditioners and the Australian Antarctic Division, a big thank you for letting me serve with you, and the opportunity to help maintain our claim on a large part of Antarctica, and the opportunity to experience such unique adventures.